THE VENGEANCE OF KYVOR

By
RANDALL GARRETT

ARMCHAIR FICTION
PO Box 4369, Medford, Oregon 97501-0168

*For more information about Armchair Books and products, visit our
website at…*

www.armchairfiction.com

Or email us at…

armchairfiction@yahoo.com

HIGH INTRIGUE IN THE JUNGLES OF VENUS...

The message from the Venusian government was clear—Earthlings stay away! However, Earth sent spaceships anyway, hoping to make contact with a brilliant Earth scientist hidden away in the Venusian jungles—a scientist who had devised a secret plan for over-throwing the cruel Venusian Empire.

But when Lanina Harrison and her brother Wayne crash-landed in the middle of a Venusian rain forest, they found themselves in the hands of a fierce tribe of tree-people. Fortunately for them, the tree-people's fiery-haired leader—known simply as Kyvor the Killer—was no friend of the Empire. Together they set out on a path that took them into direct conflict with the armed hordes of the emperor himself—a clash between the primitive forces of good and the well-armed, seemingly unstoppable forces of evil.

FOR A COMPLETE SECOND NOVEL, TURN TO PAGE 71

CAST OF CHARACTERS

KYVOR
Kyvor the Killer. His hair was red as fire, and his heart was afire for vengeance—against the cruel dictators of the Empire.

LANINA HARRISON
After crash landing on Venus, her primary concern was to find a certain jungle doctor—before the Empire scouts found her!

DR. NEILSON
A gifted Earth scientist, he had an ingenious plan for toppling the Venusian Empire. The problem was...no one could find him.

POLTHAN
This native hunter despised the Earthmen who had come to his planet, and was ready to slay them at a moment's notice.

LYMAN REEDER
He held no desire to lead an expedition into the jungle to find a fallen spaceship, but to refuse would brand him a coward.

JOHN BOCK
His scheming mind had devised a way of undermining his commander—by framing him for murder!

WAYNE HARRISON
Badly wounded in a crash landing, he soon found himself in the hands of the most fearsome natives of the jungle forest.

CHAPTER ONE

THE eternal clouds of Venus floated over the vast, murky jungle like a great blanket of gray wool, unbroken save for glimmers of pearly light filtering through from the hot sun above the endless layer of fog. Beneath, in the dense jungle itself, could be heard the whisperings of the warm breeze and the myriad voices of the life that fed and hunted in the hidden places of the great rain forest.

Polthan the Hunter crept silently along the branch of a huge Empire tree, his bare feet noiseless on the rough bark. A single misstep could plunge him helplessly into the dimness beneath, to fall a hundred feet to the ground below. Were he to do so, not even the thick moss that covered the jungle floor would save his life.

But the thought of falling never entered the mind of Polthan the Hunter. All his life had been spent in these jungles, seeking his livelihood in the leafy foliage of the vast upper reaches of the great trees. To him, the dangers that lurked on every side were as commonplace as the dangers of crossing a busy city street are to an Earthman.

Polthan's keen nostrils had detected the scent of a *glith*, a heavy, sluggish plant-eater that foraged through the heights of the jungle for the succulent leaves of the small plants that grew in the rough bark of the towering Empire trees.

Polthan's mottled blue-green skin was perfect for camouflage. Like any native Venusian, he could, by moving silently and carefully, blend so well with the foliage of the great trees that he could become completely invisible at a distance of only a few feet.

In the distance, he heard the harsh roar of a sslis reptile searching for his prey. Polthans wide, frog-like mouth smiled gently. The sslis was on the scent of the glith, too—but Polthan would reach the plant-eater first.

Then Polthan's keen ears caught another sound. It was a faint, whistling scream that became louder with every passing second. Polthan recognized the sound. It was the whine of a spaceship! It was one of the sky vessels of the despised Earthmen!

The whine became a roar as the sky ship dropped lower.

The normal jungle sounds ceased as the animals of the forest heard the terrifying sound. Polthan knew it would be of no use to try to find the glith now; it was moving rapidly away, alarmed by the scream in the air. Polthan shrugged and slung his blowgun over his shoulder. He might as well see what the Earth ship was up to.

Flexing the muscles of his legs, he leaped toward the branch above him and grasped the thick bark with the sharp, strong claws of his fingers. Thus he climbed lithely upward, from branch to branch, until he reached the top of the huge tree, hundreds of feet above the forest floor.

There, perched precariously on a swaying limb, he watched the spaceship descending rapidly through the gray Venusian sky.

Polthan knew very little of spaceships, but it was obvious, even to him, that this one was in trouble. It dropped in jerks and swayed wildly from side to side as it tried to lower itself to the solidity of the ground below.

Finally, it touched the treetops. There was a rending crash, a roar of the ship's atomic motors—then silence.

Polthan the Hunter watched for a moment, but nothing further occurred. Satisfied, he swung down from his perch and headed back toward his village. Kyvor must hear of this.

Lanina Harrison opened her eyes. For several moments, she could not recall where she was. Around her, all was dark, with the stygian blackness of a tomb. She tried to move, and a sudden, searing pain shot up her left arm, burning along her nerves like fire, wrenching a scream from her throat. The pain brought her to full consciousness.

The spaceship had crashed! And she had survived! Then the horrifying thought struck her that perhaps she was the lone survivor.

But she did not panic. Since she was sixteen, Lanina had been carefully trained by the Earth Space Service to handle herself in every emergency. From the blistering heat of Sunside Mercury to the freezing cold of Saturn's moons, Lanina Harrison had proved herself a dozen times over. Her courage had never faltered.

Nor would it falter now. Not even the dangers of the hidden surface of forbidden Venus could deter her from her purpose. Even the hideously bad luck of underestimating the armaments of the Venusian Emperor, and the resulting crash in the forest would not keep her from doing what she had been sent to Venus to do, if it lay within her power to do so.

She sat up in the darkness, being careful to put no weight on her left arm. Whether it was broken or not, she could not tell, but the throbbing pain warned her to favor it as much as she could.

"Wayne!" she shouted. "Wayne! Are you all right?"

No answer came from the pall of darkness surrounding her.

She fumbled in her jacket pocket for the tiny penlight she always carried, hoping that her fall had not damaged it. She pressed the switch and breathed a sigh of relief as the bright beam bathed the interior of the room with its radiance. She moved the beam about, trying to get her bearings.

It was quite evident that the ship had fallen on its side, for she found herself sitting on one wall.

As the spot from the brilliant beam shifted across the wall which had now become a floor, it touched that for which the girl was looking—a sprawled figure in one corner of the tipped room.

"Wayne!" Lanina gasped involuntarily.

Such was her concern for the man who lay unconscious there in the darkness of the wrecked spaceship that she ignored the pain in her arm; indeed, she almost wholly forgot it as she stood up and walked across the metal wall toward him.

He lay there unmoving, a dark bruise on his forehead showing what had happened to render him thus. Lanina put her hand on his breast, hoping against hope, fearful lest she should feel no heartbeat.

Then the tension within her relaxed. The heart beat strongly and steadily; He was only stunned; perhaps, if she could move him—

And then she saw that she could not. A heavy piece of metal, a part of the deck that had been torn loose from its fastenings during the crash, pinned one foot securely to the wall beneath him.

A low moan came from the man's lips, and he turned his head slowly from side to side.

If only there were some water! the girl thought helplessly. But she knew there was none. The wrecking of the ship had ruined the power plant, as was evidenced by the failure of the lights. Without power, the ship's replenishers could not furnish its occupants with water.

Lanina could do nothing but caress the man's cheek until time alone, allowed him to revive from the blow on his head.

After a long while, he opened his eyes and looked at her. "What—where are we?" he asked weakly.

Quickly, the girl told him what she knew of their predicament. He seemed to be in no pain; the blow of the heavy slab of metal had rendered his leg numb.

When she had finished her explanation, the man said grimly, "We might have known they'd get us, but it was our only chance. If we could only have contacted Dr. Neilson, we might have had a chance. Now, Earth will have to try again."

"Dr. Neilson is supposed to be somewhere in these jungles, Wayne. We may yet be able to contact him."

Wayne shook his head. "Not much chance. He's probably hundreds, maybe thousands, of miles away."

Lanina nodded. She realized the hopelessness of their plight, but she did not intend to show her feelings, nor did she intend to yield to despair.

"There isn't much we can do about our mission now, I'll admit," she said, "but if we ever intend to do anything; we'll have to get you out from under that deck."

"You couldn't possibly lift it by yourself," Wayne said. "And the way it has my leg pinned, I couldn't move it, either. However, I think there is a way. You'll have to get the hydraulic lifter out of the engine room and get the deck up that way. It needs to be lifted only a few inches."

"I think that's the best way," the girl agreed. She turned around and pointed the flashlight's beam toward the wall where a door opened into the engine room.

"I can never get through that door!" she said in dismay. The metal of the wall had been warped in the accident, and the door itself was twisted in such a way that it was jammed tightly in the opening.

"I can see that," Wayne said. "It would take more force to open that door than it would to lift this deck. You'll have to go outside the ship and enter the engine room from the emergency hatch." A grimace of pain crossed his handsome face. "You'd better hurry," he continued, "my leg's beginning to hurt; the numbness is wearing off."

"I'll be back as soon as possible," she assured him.

It was fortunate that the ship had not landed on the side where the airlock was situated, or Lanina could never have made her way out of the smashed metal hulk. As it was, the port opened easily, and as it swung in, Lanina saw for the first time the misty beauty of the Venusian jungle.

Everywhere she looked there were great flowers, hanging from the thick, cable-like vines that looped through the branches of the trees. Against the dark, blue-green of the foliage, they stood out as bright spots of color.

Reds, blues, greens, yellows and purples sparkled brilliantly, while pastel shades of chartreuse, pink, lemon, and pale orange added their glowing softness to the panorama of color.

Never in her life, Lanina thought, had she seen anything to compare with the beauty around her.

Then her eyes looked down, and a shiver of terror coursed over her body. Below the airlock door, there was no solid ground—only a leafy, blue-green abyss that dropped into dimness and mist far below. She knew, then, what had happened. The spaceship had not fallen to the jungle floor; it had come to rest on two mighty branches of a gigantic Empire tree!

One of the great branches, easily twelve feet thick and covered with the heavy, blossoming vines, supported the tail end of the battered spaceship; another, equally large, held the nose. There was no way she could get out of the ship!

To attempt to climb around on the smooth hull of the vessel, even with magnetic shoes, would have been foolhardy; the magnets were never meant to hold a human body against the pull of gravity; they were meant for gravityless action in the depths of space. And if she were to fall—

She shuddered again as she looked down into the empty depths below her.

How could she get to the engine room now? There was no way; she would have to think of some other method of freeing Wayne from the imprisoning weight of the massive metal deck.

A noise to her right brought her attention from the emptiness beneath the ship. She looked up, and what she saw made her voice a gasping cry.

Standing on a branch not ten feet from the open door of the spaceship were two things that looked like demons from some horrid nightmare. Short of stature they were, not more than four feet tall, with mottled blue-green skin and short, muscular limbs that bespoke great strength in spite of the diminutive size of the beings. Their mouths were wide and filled with small, pointed teeth. Above the mouth were two small nostrils, mere openings in a noseless face. The eyes were large and luminous and somehow managed to convey an impression of intelligence and craft.

In spite of their upright posture and large, well-shaped foreheads, Lanina could not help thinking that they looked like huge frogs.

She had seen photographs of Venusian natives before, but they were more frightening in reality than their photographs could ever be. Still, she forced down her terror and, remembering that some of the natives could understand English, she called out to them.

"I am a friend. My brother is hurt. I need help. Please!"

Neither of the Venusians said a word, nor did they give any sign that they understood the tongue of the Earth girl.

Then another thought occurred to her. Dr. Neilson, the man she and Wayne were supposed to contact, had worked in these jungles for thirty years. Perhaps if she asked for him, they might give some sign, for it was known that Dr. Neilson was friendly with many of the natives.

"Do you know Dr. Neilson?" she asked. "We are friends of Dr. Neilson's. Doc-tor *Neil*-son." She repeated the name in hopes that the natives might recognize it, even if they understood no other English.

And indeed they did show signs of understanding, for they glanced at each other and one of them spoke in the rippling, fluid tongue of Venus.

But before the other could answer, another voice came.

"What about Dr. Neilson?" asked a deep, authoritative voice.

Lanina turned her head to see who had spoken and stared wide-eyed in surprise. Standing on another nearby branch was a tall, magnificently handsome man—an Earthman! He was almost naked; only a loincloth of soft, yellow-green fur covered his golden skin. He was taller than any man she had ever seen before, taller even than Wayne, and his shoulders were broad and powerfully muscled. The eyes that looked at her from beneath his frowning brows were a deep, cool blue. But the most outstanding thing about this handsome, golden giant was the flaming red hair that was brushed back from his high forehead in smooth waves.

"I asked you a question," he said calmly. "What about Dr. Neilson?"

CHAPTER TWO

KYVOR the Killer lay on his back, gazing indolently at the shifting silvery gray of the Venusian skies. The rough bark of the mighty tree limb upon which he reposed felt pleasant to his golden skin, and the warm, humid breeze, which caressed his face, enhanced the feeling of lassitude that had stolen over his muscular body.

And yet, relaxed though he may be, the keen senses of Kyvor the Killer were ever alert for danger. The reptilian predators that crept through the Venusian rain forest were silent and insidious in their movements, and only a trained ear could detect their presence; only nostrils of utmost delicacy could tell their scent from the myriad of other aromas that permeated the moist air. And only by hard, never-ceasing training from childhood could an Earthman hope to stay alive in the jungles of Venus without elaborate protective equipment.

Thus it was that when Kyvor heard the faint rasp of callused feet on the bark of a nearby branch, his every muscle was ready for instant action. But he did not leap to his feet, for his sensitive nostrils told him that the one who approached was a member of the Clan of Tivala. Indeed, it was only a few seconds later that the smiling figure of Polthan the Hunter stepped into view from behind a screen of leafy foliage.

"Good hunting, mighty Flame-head," said Polthan, using the customary Venusian greeting, and addressing the Earthman by his Venusian name. The name "Kyvor" means, literally, "He-who-has-flame-on-his-head," for the Clan of Tivala, as the natives call themselves, have no hair; and not even the furred animals have hair that is red or brown.

"Good hunting, Polthan," returned Kyvor. "You seem to be excited—more excited, I dare say, than the mere killing of a glith would warrant."

Polthan's thick lips split in a broad smile, disclosing the rows of small, sharp teeth. "Indeed, it is so, mighty Kyvor," Polthan said. "Did you not hear the scream in the jungle?"

"I heard it," Kyvor admitted, "but it sounded like a dying sslis."

"Not nearby," Polthan corrected, shaking his head. "I know you have never heard the sound in your life, but we of Tivala who are older heard it often in years gone by. It was a spaceship landing."

Kyvor leaped to his feet. "Where? Take me there quickly, Polthan! If they are agents of the Empire, they will bear close watching."

"I think we need have no fear, Kyvor," said Polthan; "the vessel was out of control and crashed. No doubt the occupants were killed."

"If you did not investigate, you can not know," Kyvor said. "Come, show me the ship."

Polthan nodded quickly and scurried off through the trees, running along branches, and leaping the gaps between the great trees by swinging along the cable-like vines that festooned the limbs in the upper forest. Behind him, with equal ease, sped Kyvor the Killer.

As he moved through the jungle, Kyvor's keen mind dwelt on the possibilities of a spaceship here in the jungle.

It had been very long since the young giant had set eyes on his own kind. Since the death of his parents, years before, he had not seen a human being. His only friends, his people, were the Clan of Tivala. He had been only a child when his mother had at last succumbed to fever, weakened by the despair in her heart after the murder of her husband, Kyvor's father.

Even then, child though he had been, he was as large, physically, as the greatest warrior of the Clan. And the Clans people had adopted him, teaching him those things that a young warrior needs to know in the rain forest of Venus. He knew what plants to avoid, and which plants could be useful to him. He had learned how to kill the herbivorous glith and protect himself from the fierce, ravenous attacks of the sslis.

And as he had grown to young manhood, he had become stronger and more agile than any of the Clan, and their primitive minds had come to look upon him as a god-king, rather than as a simple chieftain. The books and papers of his father he had read and re-read until everything in that vast library was engraved permanently in his facile mind.

And now, for the first time in years, he might again see a human face. Perhaps, as Polthan had said, they were dead; perhaps, as he himself surmised, they were agents of the Empire. But they were nonetheless human, and Kyvor felt, deep within his savage breast, the desire to see a human being once again.

Polthan felt a little ashamed that he had been chastised by Kyvor. Was it not sensible to assume that anything falling from so great a height would kill those within it? Polthan thought so, and yet Kyvor knew more of such things, even though he had never seen a spaceship. Kyvor had many "books" which spoke to him silently when he looked at them, and they told him many wise things. The arts of writing and reading were beyond the intellect of Polthan's people.

Since Kyvor had cast doubt upon the death of the vessel's occupants, then it was extremely likely that it must be so. Therefore, Polthan reasoned, it *must* be so.

The people of the Clan of Tivala, though ignorant of the complexities of Earth's civilization, were wise in the equally complex ways of the jungle. The rapid movement of Kyvor and the faithful Polthan through the upper reaches of the great forest did not go unnoticed by its denizens, nor had the falling of the spaceship been observed by Polthan alone. Thus it was that when Kyvor and his guide reached the spot where the broken ship hung in the tree, many of the Tivala were gathered around it, keeping well hidden in the greenery that surrounded the ship.

Mylthat the Trapper hurried over to where Kyvor stood watching the ship.

"We have seen nothing, Fiery One," he whispered, "but there have been noises within the vessel, clangings of metal upon metal."

Polthan nodded. "They are alive, of course," he said. "We shall kill them when they emerge."

Mylthat clenched his hand around his short-spear. "As soon as they open the round door, they die."

Kyvor the Killer had been surveying the disabled ship, ignoring the low conversation of the two Tivala, but when Mylthat shook his short-spear, the tall Earthman looked down at him. "No, Mylthat, that will not be necessary. They cannot get out of the ship; there are no vines close enough to allow them to climb out, since they were torn out by the ship's fall. And, even should they manage to get out, it would be better to wait until they are all out, where they will be more vulnerable to our weapons."

"It is as Kyvor says," agreed Polthan.

"Listen!" Kyvor's voice carried a tone of command. "One of them is opening the airlock! Silence!"

At his order, the Clan of Tivala became motionless and silent. Following their leader's command they waited.

Kyvor thought himself ready for anything, but he was totally unprepared for the door to swing inward and disclose the face of a beautiful, golden-haired girl.

He could tell that she was frightened, but the nobility and beauty of her soft oval face impressed him deeply. It was difficult to believe that such a lovely creature could be an agent of the Empire. But what else could she be?

The girl looked around her in wonder for a few moments, then looked down at the vast open space beneath her and gasped. She seemed fascinated by the sheer depth of the leafy, blue-green abyss.

"Quickly!" Kyvor whispered to the two standing beside him; "go out to the branch near her while she is not looking. Do nothing and say nothing. Just stand where she can see you."

Then he gave orders to the others while Polthan and Mylthat scurried to do his bidding. "Aim your blowguns at the girl; if she attempts to harm Polthan or Mylthat, kill her."

It was an order he did not like to give; the beauty and apparent innocence of the girl did not bespeak evil intent. But she was nonetheless an enemy, or at least a stranger, while the two Tivala were his friends.

When the girl looked up at last and saw the two Tivala standing before her, Kyvor was again forced to grudging admiration of her bravery. She did not run back into the ship, nor did she draw a weapon. Instead, she spoke, and her voice was clear and soft, without the slightest trace of fear.

"I am a friend. My brother is hurt. I need help. Please!"

Kyvor narrowed his eyes. It might be a trap, but if so, it was a crude one. Besides, the girl's voice had a ring of sincerity. Still, if they were agents of the Empire, there was no need to save their lives; they would only become dangerous later. And yet, there were many questions to be answered. Why had they come here? What were they looking for? Why had the ship crashed?

The girl's voice came again. "Do you know Dr. Neilson? We are friends of Dr. Neilson's. Doc-tor *Neil*-son."

At her mention of that name, Kyvor decided that he would have to take personal hand in dealing with the girl. He strode out on a nearby branch and folded his arms over his chest. "What about Dr. Neilson?" he asked.

The startled girl turned her head to look at him, and her gray eyes grew wide with fear and surprise. She said nothing, so Kyvor repeated his question.

"We—we've come to see him," the girl replied. "Who are you?"

"I am known as Kyvor," he said simply. "Why do you want to see Dr. Neilson? Who are you?"

The girl had claimed to be a friend of Dr. Neilson's, and Kyvor well knew that she had never met the doctor.

Lanina Harrison paused. She had no idea who this golden giant might be; he could very well be an agent of the Venusian Empire, in which case it would be foolish and dangerous to reveal the identity of herself and her brother. And yet, the spaceship itself was real and damaging evidence against her. The handsome demigod must know that she did not come from Empire City.

"Our ship was damaged," she said at last. "We were forced to land here, and we knew that Dr. Neilson's headquarters were in this area. We thought perhaps he could help us."

"You speak of 'we,'" Kyvor said. "Who else is aboard?"

He knew that there was something odd about the girl's story, but he had correctly deduced that she intended to tell him nothing, so he asked her nothing more about herself.

"Only my brother and I are aboard," she said. "He's inside; his leg has been crushed under a piece of deck, and he can't move. Please, if you have any kindness about you, help us!"

Kyvor paused for only a moment. Well he knew that there might be danger within the ship, but his instinct told him that the girl was telling the truth. He grasped a vine, and with one graceful leap swung over the open space to the lip of the airlock.

"Take me to your brother," he said.

Lanina led him back to where Wayne Harrison lay in the darkness of the ship. He did not move, nor did he speak when Lanina called out his name; he had fainted again from the pain in his leg.

From the illumination of the girl's flashlight, Kyvor could see that the young man bore a striking resemblance to his sister, although his face was more angular and masculine.

Lanina watched as Kyvor walked over to the metal deck plate and grasped it with one hand. She saw his mighty thews ripple under the golden skin, and the deck lifted as easily as if it were made of cardboard. With his free hand, Kyvor gently moved the injured man's foot from beneath the mass of metal. Then he lowered the deck again, and without another word, he picked up the unconscious man in his arms and strode toward the airlock. Lanina followed him, not knowing what else to do or what to expect.

CHAPTER THREE

SEVERAL hundred miles to the north of the spot where the spaceship had landed, a gigantic military transport ship landed in an open jungle area, depositing a column of troops and armored vehicles. Four heavy armored tanks lumbered southward. The column moved in single file, their headlights gleaming in the misty dimness of the jungle floor.

In the lead tank, Major Lyman Reeder, of the Imperial Venusian Army, scowled darkly and cursed venomously under his breath.

"Why so angry, Major?" asked Captain Bock, second in command.

"I don't like the idea of bringing a nurse along," the Major said. "Women don't belong on a military expedition. They are always and forever in the way. We needed a doctor, yes. But not a nurse."

That was not the real reason for the Major's anger, although it irritated him. Actually, he had no real desire to be heading a military expedition into the jungle. He would much rather have stayed in Empire City, making the rounds of the cafes, attending the various social functions of Imperial society. He thoroughly disliked the idea of plunging into the unknown depths of the Venusian jungles. There was, of course, nothing he could do about it; had he begged off, he would have been disgraced and called a coward in the social circles of Empire City. In fact, it was doubtful that he could have begged off; the order to find the fallen spaceship, and capture prisoners if possible, had come straight from the Emperor himself, and Derek II was not a monarch who rescinded his personal orders.

Major Reeder had to go, but he most certainly did not have to like it. Therefore, his disposition was irritable and his treatment of the men under him harsh.

Captain John Bock didn't object; as a matter of fact, he was rather glad that he had been assigned to the expedition. He knew that the Emperor was anxious to capture whoever had been in the mysterious ship, and he was determined that he would get his share of the credit for the success of the expedition. Well he knew the weaknesses of his commander, and he intended to take every advantage of them.

"Why do you think the ship came here, sir?" the captain asked conversationally.

"Who knows?" snapped the Major. "I can tell you this, though, any ship from Earth is a potential danger to the Empire. Ever since Derek I declared Venus to be separate from the government of Earth, we have known that the President of Earth would do everything in his power to see that the Empire is destroyed. The democratic earthlings claim that a government by aristocracy is despotic. Bah! Can you imagine a world where the common rabble is permitted a voice in the government? There can be no such thing."

"It does seem foolish in the extreme," Captain Bock agreed. "Our ancestors, who colonized Venus, were wise to cut themselves loose from the bonds that tied them to a decadent society."

The Major, who knew nothing of history and cared even less, merely snorted. "Nevertheless," he said, "Earth has always been a threat to us, and always will be until its society collapses into anarchy."

Captain Bock nodded in agreement, but he privately disagreed with Major Reeder. The Empire controlled the spots on Venus where a spaceship could land: the broad, flat salt plains of the North. All the rest was jungle, swamps, and mountains. Earth could not possibly land a fleet of ships to invade, since the heavy blaster guns could shoot them out of the sky before they could touch the ground. Neither could they bomb the Empire from space, for the heavy blasters could hit a bomb as easily as a spaceship. Earth could win only by destroying the whole planet, and there would be no point in doing that.

He wondered, nevertheless, why this lone ship had come from Earth. What could they hope to accomplish? The ship had attempted to land in the great marshes just out of range of the blasters; but they had underestimated the range of the huge guns, and a near hit had disabled them. They had fled to the south, only to crash into the vast rain forest. Whoever had been aboard her would most certainly have died in the crash, but, even so, there would be clues aboard her that might disclose her purpose in coming here.

While the captain pondered thusly, the column of tanks moved on over the thick moss that covered the jungle floor. Like four tiny ants crawling around the vast pillars of a cathedral, they wound their torturous way through the towering Empire trees. The great forest monarchs, some of them a full quarter of a mile in diameter, seemed to ignore the small crawling things beneath them as a man would ignore an insect at his feet.

On and on they moved through the dimness of the jungle until at last the pearly light in the sky began to fade and the utter blackness of the Venusian night settled over them. Not until then did the Major call a halt.

The four tanks were formed into a hollow square, and the space between them was blocked with heavy steel fencing. Outside this, an electrical barrier was set up which would kill any small animal and stun or frighten larger ones. Powerful searchlights were set up to illuminate the area, and sentries were posted around the camp. Then the soldiers made ready to eat their evening meal and retire until morning.

In one corner of the compound, a special tent had been set up, and Major Reeder eyed it with open dislike.

"That," he said to Captain Bock, "is exactly what I mean when I say that a woman is a nuisance on a military expedition. She has to have special attention, special quarters, special everything.

"Captain, I'm going to make her your responsibility. I would just as soon she didn't bother me."

"Yes, sir," replied the captain. "I'll see that she doesn't annoy you." Inwardly, he smiled at his superior's order. He hadn't dared to hope that he would have such luck; his scheming mind had already worked out a way to undermine his commanding officer and take credit for the expedition himself. Because he knew that the young nurse was already angry with the Major's tyrannical methods, he hoped to use her in his scheme, and the Major's order fell in with his plans. And, too, he had other plans for the girl herself.

Excusing himself from the Major's company, he strolled across the compound toward the nurse's tent. When he reached it, he tapped on the aluminum frame of the door to the tent.

"Who is it?" came a clear contralto voice from within.

"Captain Bock," said the officer. "May I come in?"

"Certainly, Captain," said the nurse. She was seated at a table with Captain Ashley, the elderly medical officer.

Bock had expected to find the girl alone, and he was somewhat discomfited to see them both.

"Good evening, Lieutenant Summers; Captain Ashley; I hope you're both comfortable. How did the first day go?"

"Not badly," replied Captain Ashley, "although I must say riding in a tank with nine other men is not my idea of comfort."

"I hope my men didn't bother you," said Bock. "If they do, I shall see that they are disciplined."

Dora Summers looked up at the young captain. He might have been handsome, except for the cruelty in his dark eyes, which showed through in spite of the engaging smile on his face.

"Your men didn't bother me, Captain," she said. "They seem very well trained."

"As well trained as it is possible to train peasants," Captain Bock agreed.

Nurse Summers said nothing. Not by so much as a flicker of her lustrous brown eyes did she betray the thought that passed through her mind.

Captain Ashley stretched his arms wide. "I'm really getting too old for this sort of thing," he said. "Frankly, I doubt that a doctor will be needed. If the crash didn't kill the people in the spaceship, I dare say they'll be dead by the time we get there. An unprotected human being can't last long in the jungles of Venus." He yawned and stood up. "Frankly, I'm going to get some sleep—I need it. Goodnight."

Captain Bock and the nurse bade him goodnight as he pushed open the door of the aluminum-cloth tent and went out to his own quarters.

As soon as he had gone, Captain Bock turned again to the nurse. "The Major was rather harsh with you this morning, wasn't he?"

Lieutenant Summers just shrugged her smooth shoulders. "He's the commanding officer here. I have to take orders like anyone else."

"True," the captain agreed, "but I think he's much too overbearing with everyone. Even a common soldier has some rights." He looked searchingly into the dark, soft eyes of the woman. "If you want my opinion, I think we need a psychiatrist along instead of a medical doctor."

Dora Summers met his gaze steadily, and she, too, was attempting to read the brain behind those eyes. "Do you mean that you think Major Reeder is insane?"

The captain laughed and shook his head. "No, Dora, I didn't say that. You did. However, I won't disagree with you. Perhaps—" His smile faded, and he left the sentence unfinished.

He rose from his seat, said goodnight, and left. Dora Summers watched him leave and wondered what sort of man the captain really was. Could she trust him? She felt that she had to trust someone, but what would Captain Bock's reaction be if he discovered that she was not the well-born lady she claimed to be, but only a commoner? She did not know, and until she could be more sure of the young officer, she decided it would be more prudent to hold her tongue.

Restless, she stood up and walked outside the tent to take a breath of fresh air. The humidity of the jungle breeze seemed to be less in the evening.

Around her she could see nothing except the camp itself. Beyond the glare of the brilliant spotlights, there seemed to be nothing but impenetrable darkness.

Thus, she could not see the pair of large, glowing eyes that sought her out in the glare of the lights, eyes that watched from the jungle and remained fastened upon the door to her aluminum tent after she had gone inside and shut off the light.

CHAPTER FOUR

LANINA HARRISON massaged the wrist of her left hand. There was little pain in it, but a slight tenderness remained. Fortunately, it had only been a slight sprain.

Wayne, on the other hand, had not had his sister's good luck. His foot had been broken, and only the skill of their unknown benefactor had saved the limb. As it was, Kyvor had set the fracture so well that Wayne was able to hobble about on a pair of crutches without paining himself too much.

At the moment, he was seated on a rude, but serviceable couch that stood against one wall of the room where they stayed.

"It just doesn't seem possible," Wayne said as he looked about him; "to think that we're actually inside a tree!"

"Kyvor says that the Empire trees are filled with such hollows as this," Lanina said. "The natives widen them and polish the inside walls to give them the finish."

Indeed, the room, primitive though it might be, had an air of grandeur about it, for the walls looked as though they were made of paneled mahogany, smoothly varnished and polished to a high luster. It was a large room, and yet, in comparison, it was only a tiny scar in the vast bulk of the mighty tree.

There was a rustling at the entranceway, and a huge hand pulled aside the bark-cloth that concealed the entrance from outside eyes.

The flame-haired giant smiled as he stepped inside the tree-cavern room. "How do you feel, Wayne? Foot still hurt?"

"I think it's all right," the Earthman said. "Still throbs a little, but what can you expect of a broken leg?"

Kyvor seemed to be enjoying some private joke, which neither of the others understood. They had told him that they were merely citizens of Empire City who were trying to test a new type of spaceship. Something had gone wrong, they said, and the ship had crashed. Otherwise, they had told him nothing.

And, in return, Kyvor had asked them nothing. He had no need to; his eyes and his ears told him more than the two Earthlings suspected. He knew by their slight accents that they had not come from Empire City; more, he could see that their clothing, although cut in the Empire style, were not made on Venus. His keen eyes could detect subtle differences in the cut and make of the cloth that would go unnoticed to ordinary human eyes. Long years in the Venusian jungles had sharpened his senses far beyond those of the average man.

"Well," he said quietly, "I suppose you're ready, now, to be taken to Empire City. You'll want to get back home."

Lanina and her brother glanced at each other, and the message that passed between them did not pass unnoticed by the golden-skinned giant, who smiled slightly to himself.

Suddenly, he could contain himself no longer. Kyvor's vast sense of humor bubbled over and he began laughing at the plight of the two before him.

"I'm sorry," he said at last, when his laughter had subsided. "I didn't mean to frighten you. But why didn't you tell me you were Earth agents? Was it because you thought I was an agent of the so-called Venusian Empire? What Empire man would stay out here in the jungle when he could have the comforts of the city?"

Wayne Harrison smoothed back his blond hair with a muscular hand. "Then you've known all along?"

Kyvor nodded. "Ever since I first heard you speak. And, too, the evidence aboard the ship shows that it isn't of Venusian origin. Besides, you asked about Dr. Neilson; that was a dead giveaway, in itself. Everyone on Venus knows that Dr. Neilson is dead."

Young Harrison looked at the fire-haired young giant in astonishment. "Dead? But he assured Earth that he was in no danger; he said that he could stay away from the Empire's police forever, if necessary."

Kyvor nodded. "He was right. But there was more to it than that. Let me tell you what I know, then you can tell me what has taken place on Earth.

"Twenty years ago, Neilson contacted Earth. He had a plan for allowing Earth forces to land to overthrow the Empire and free the so called 'commoners' from the slavery of the Empire's aristocrats and set up a democratic government on Venus. For five years, he carried on radio communication with Earth. Then communication was stopped, but Neilson assured Earth that there was nothing wrong. Since then he has not been heard from."

Lanina said, "That's right. We were sent to contact Neilson; there was hope that he was still alive. His last message told us that he needed new supplies for his radio, that some of the transistors were nearly burned out. No further messages were received, but it was assumed that the doctor had simply been unable to get new supplies. Finally, after fifteen years, the Earth decided that if one ship could get through to him, we could help him bring his plan about. Unfortunately—"

"Unfortunately," finished Kyvor, "you didn't know two things. You didn't know that the small landing field he told you of was now occupied by the Empire, and you didn't know that he had been killed. This changes your plans.

"In order to get parts for his radio, he stole secretly into Empire City, the only place where they could be had. He was captured and tortured to death. But he died without revealing his headquarters." When he said this last, the flashing blue eyes of Kyvor became as cold as the blue ice of Earth's Arctic.

"Do you know where his headquarters were?" Lanina asked.

Kyvor nodded. "I do," he said. "I am the only living human being who does know. The things he worked with should never fall into the hands of the Emperor of Venus. Derek II would become a tyrant, the like of which has never been seen, if the secrets in Dr. Neilson's laboratory were to become his."

Wayne Harrison's gray eyes blazed with sudden interest. "How do you know so much, Kyvor? Who are you, anyway?"

"My real name is Glen Neilson," Kyvor said quietly. "I am Dr. Neilson's son." He stopped a moment, remembering. Then he said, "I have lived in these jungles all my life. I was reared by the Clan of Tivala. I am the only Earthman who is not hated by the tree people of Venus."

The red-haired young giant had no further opportunity to explain his background. A small, blue-green figure darted into the room and spoke in the rippling tongue of the Clan of Tivala. The Earthlings could understand no word of it, but they could easily see the excitement of the speaker.

When he had finished and scampered out again, Kyvor spoke to the Earthman. "Wayne, the Empire has spotted the place where your ship crashed. Even now, there is a column of tanks coming through the forest toward us. Polthan the Hunter says that they are only a day away."

Wayne's heavy blond brows furrowed in thought. "They'll find the ship, of course; their detectors will tell them where it is. And they'll know we're alive. When they report back—"

"Don't worry about that," Kyvor said. "I'll see to it that they don't report back." He stood up and strode out the door of the tree cave.

Lanina Harrison sprang to her feet and rushed out after him. "Kyvor! Wait! What are you going to do?" When she had left the room, she had run out on the mighty branch that projected out from beneath the hole in the bark; but she took no notice of that, for the branch was fully ten feet thick and therefore easy to walk on without losing balance.

Kyvor turned to look at her. "What am I going to do? I'm going to get rid of an enemy patrol. I've done it before; there's nothing to fear."

The Earth girl reached out and touched him gently with one hand. "Don't—don't get hurt." And then, suddenly, she threw her arms about him and lay her head against his mighty chest. "Please be careful! Please!"

"He's been gone for hours," said Lanina Harrison, pacing back and forth across the room.

"Relax, honey," Wayne told her. "That man knows his way around these jungles. He's stayed alive this long; he'll stay alive a lot longer." He looked up at his sister knowingly. "You've fallen in love with the guy, haven't you?"

Lanina turned, her eyes blazing. "Well, what if I have? Can you imagine anyone better to fall in love with?"

Wayne shook his head. "No, I can't," he confessed. "The man's magnificent. But—does he love you?"

Lanina clenched her fists and closed her eyes. "I don't know," she said softly. "I don't know."

Wayne stood up on his crutches and hobbled across the room. "I hate to disillusion you, honey, but I think you ought to take everything into account before you make any decision." He pushed open the door to the next room, the one where Kyvor slept. "Come here, Lanina. Kyvor talked with me for a while in here. I know I'm intruding on his privacy to show you this, but I think you should know." He flung the door open wide and pointed within. The flickering glow of the oil lamps, which illuminated the hidden recesses within the tree, glowed fitfully over the far wall of the room. And there, Lanina could see a life-size photograph of a young, dark-haired, brown-eyed, beautiful girl.

And, inscribed beneath it were the words, "To Kyvor, with all my love."

Kyvor the Killer raced through the branches of the upper terrace, moving steadily and unerringly toward the place where the tank column had been spotted. He took with him no provisions, for they would only serve to slow his rapid pace through the jungle. His only necessities were the knife and rope that hung at his side; he could live off the land as well as any other inhabitant of the Venusian rain forest, and, indeed, preferred to do so.

When Dr. Simon Neilson, one of the most brilliant scientists who had ever lived, had fled into the jungles of Venus to keep his secrets out of the hands of the despotic Empire, he had taken with him his wife and small son. Since early childhood, young Glen had been raised and taught by the Clan of Tivala, with whom his scientist father had become friendly. While Dr. Neilson worked in his hidden laboratory, Kyvor, the Fire Hair, had played with the young Tivala children and learned their ways.

Then Simon Neilson had gone back to Empire City for badly needed equipment, and had never returned. Shortly thereafter, his beloved mother had succumbed to fever and loneliness, leaving Kyvor in the hands of the faithful people of the Clan of Tivala. And they had not failed in their duty; day by day and year by year they had taught the lad the secrets of the jungle, secrets he needed in order to survive. The boy had learned well; indeed, because of his superior brain, he soon surpassed his instructors, until now the Clan looked upon the young giant as one almost akin to the gods.

Knowing his father's hatred for the Empire, and knowing how they had killed him and indirectly caused the death of his mother, an intense hatred of the Empire had been instilled in Kyvor's own mind. Often they had sent patrols and expeditions into the jungle, and each time Kyvor heard of one, he had proceeded as he was proceeding now—to wipe it out.

Perhaps, Kyvor reflected, it was not quite right to think of Lanina and her brother as the only humans he had seen since his parents' death. Still, it was only with effort that he could bring himself to think of the soldiers of the Emperor as being human. Their savagery and cruelty were such that they scarcely deserved the honor of being called men.

Never once on these expeditions had he spoken to one of the soldiers. He had killed them by using his vast knowledge of the jungle, and left their bodies to the mercies of the carnivores and carrion eaters of the jungle. When all was over, the machines were left to rust, while the winged dak-lizards swooped ever lower toward the corpses, and the small, jackal-like thelks crept out of the underbrush to feed.

CHAPTER FIVE

THAT evening, Kyvor slowed his steady movement through the jungle and began to search for food for his evening repast. The faithful Polthan swung by his side through the heavy vines of the forest, sniffing the air with his flat nostrils.

Suddenly Kyvor changed direction, veering off sharply to the right. Polthan followed, for he, too, had scented the glith.

The big beast, hanging upside-down from a limb, moved slowly along, munching leaves and flowers from the liana vines. Kyvor and Polthan crept up silently and watched. Great care must be taken to catch glith. If he is killed outright, he will simply fall, hundreds of feet, to the jungle floor below. Before a hunter could reach him, the flesh would be despoiled by the thousands of tiny, thumb-sized carrion beetles that rush from their burrows in the moss whenever anything edible falls from above. The little eaters of dead could burrow into a body within a few seconds, rendering it unfit for consumption because of the noxious secretions of their bodies.

Thus it was that the glith had to be taken by more subtle means.

Carefully unreeling his rope, Kyvor prepared a noose, and with unerring accuracy threw it over the blunt, thick-necked head of the browsing monster. Immediately, the animal reached out with one great claw and began to tear at the offending strand of rope.

Then Kyvor leaped. Grasping the animal with one mighty arm about his throat, Kyvor plunged his knife again and again into its side, searching for the huge heart that beat beneath the protective hide.

Screaming with pain, the great beast released his hold on the branch and dropped. But the rope that Kyvor had fastened to a higher branch held, and the fall was stopped as abruptly as it had begun as the glith jerked helplessly at the end of the rope.

Still the great animal did not die. Tough were his great neck muscles, and strong the will to live within his heart. His great tree-holding talons slashed back, trying to dislodge the human from his back. But Kyvor was not to be cheated of his prey. His powerful arms and legs held their grip about the glith's body, and his knife sought once more the heart of the beast.

The glith's motions began to become more sluggish, and at last it moved no more. Then, hand over hand, his bloody knife clenched between his teeth, Kyvor the Killer climbed up the rope which held the huge body suspended from the limb above.

As soon as he had reached the limb, he began pulling up the glith and before long, he and Polthan were tearing with their teeth at the raw chunks of flesh that had been hacked off the dead herbivore.

After they had sated themselves, the giant Earthman and the small Venusian found a small cavern in the trunk of a nearby tree and lodged themselves for the night there to rest and wait.

Lieutenant Dora Summers pointed at the drug cabinet and said, "I tell you, Dr. Ashley, someone has been taking llomar powder from the drug supply!"

Captain Ashley looked at the calibrated vials and nodded. "You're right, Nurse. There's a good deal of it missing. When did you first notice that it was gone?"

"Just a few minutes ago," the nurse replied. "Just before I called you."

The physician frowned. "I couldn't believe it at first," he said. "I can't see why anyone would want to take it. It's not a narcotic, nor a stimulant. Why would anyone want to steal the llomar drug?"

Lieutenant Summers was almost sure she knew, but it was not her business to make wild guesses. She merely asked, "It's a poison, isn't it?"

Dr. Ashley nodded. "Yes, but not in the usual sense. It attacks the nerves, and specifically attacks the cerebrum—the thinking part of the brain."

The two of them were standing in the hospital hut, on the fourth night out from Empire City. The journey had been slow and monotonous; the dreadful tales they had heard about the dangers of the Venusian rain forest had not seemed to have come true. Instead of deadly danger, there was only the utter sameness of the unchanging jungle.

"I suppose I had better notify Major Reeder," Captain Ashley said thoughtfully. "Steps will have to be taken to insure against further losses."

Dora watched as the captain walked across the compound. She knew in her heart that only one man could have stolen the llomar powder.

Captain Ashley rapped on the door of the Major's tent. At the sound of the voice that bade him come in, he pushed open the door—

—*and was confronted by a madman!*

Major Lyman Reeder was foaming at the mouth; his eyes were wild and red—bloodshot with hate.

"Aha! There you are!" he cackled madly. "I'm going to kill you, you know! Ha ha! I'm going to kill you!"

Dr. Ashley knew then what had happened to the llomar drug—someone had given it to Major Reeder!

He could hardly manage to get out of the insane man's way. It was too late! The Major was charging straight for him, and the captain couldn't possibly avoid him in time!

Lanina Harrison looked over at the couch where her brother was sleeping soundly. She was glad that the pain in his foot had subsided at last to the point where he could sleep, but she was worried about Kyvor. What had happened to the red-haired giant? He had been gone now nearly two days. Had the Empire soldiers killed him? Or had he met some worse fate?

She could not know. The tiny green Venusians could not tell her, for they spoke no English; and she, in turn, was unable to speak the tongue of the Clan of Tivala. But, she decided, she must know what had happened to the golden-skinned man who had won her love.

Quietly, she walked over to the crude desk, which stood on squat legs in one corner of the room. Dipping the ancient steel pen in ink, she wrote a few lines. Then she put the piece of paper on Wayne's chest, where he would be sure to see it when he awoke.

Then, buckling her weapon belt around her slim waist, she stepped outside and began to walk quietly along the wide branch of the great tree.

All around her glowed the phosphorescent flowers of the great vines, shimmering in their various colors in the blackness of the Venusian night. They stored the light that fell upon them by day and glowed at night, filling the darkness with a soft light that was just barely enough to see by, provided one had exceptionally keen vision.

Lanina had a keen sense of direction. Although she was by no means trained to live in the jungle, she nevertheless was capable of acting in an emergency; and her senses were, in spite of their comparative weakness, still a great deal better than the average man's. So, stepping carefully along the branches, she moved toward the spaceship that had crashed far off in the jungle.

She walked carefully; she could not hope to equal the daring swings across space that Kyvor performed with such apparent ease and daring; but, nonetheless, she did not feel afraid as she walked along, jumping from one branch to another, making long detours where an easy jump was not feasible.

She could not, however, hope to equal the silence of Kyvor. Her every step made the bark beneath her feet crackle. She tried to steal along quietly, but her heavy, solid space boots made the bark crunch every time she shifted her weight. But to her, this was of little consequence. She could hear it only slightly, and naively assumed that no other denizen of the jungle could hear better than she could. She did not know that before she had moved twenty yards there were others in the trees who watched her with glowing eyes and followed her silently. Amid the shining liana blossoms the eyes could not be seen, but they watched and moved, nonetheless.

It took her a long time to navigate her way through the upper terrace. In half an hour, she had covered a distance that would have taken a Venusian child less than five minutes.

She knew that the tank column had spotted the place where her ship had crashed, and she knew that Kyvor, if he were still alive, would be somewhere near the wreckage.

Sense of direction though she had, Lanina knew nothing of the dangers that surrounded her. Although the motions and sounds in the jungle disturbed her, she did not know what they were, and the distant hissing roar of a sslis meant nothing to her. She could not know that the reptilian carnivore had scented her and was already moving cautiously toward her after giving his single hunting warning.

Distant as he was, the reptile nonetheless moved through his familiar surroundings much more rapidly than the prey ahead. He paused now and then, sniffing the air, trying to decide just what sort of animal it was that lay ahead. It really did not matter to the sslis, for in his tiny brain there was no room for fear; he did not know what it was, but he knew that it was food, and he knew that he was a match for any animal that roamed the forest. On and on he pressed, moving with a cat-like grace that no terrestrial reptile ever achieved. For the Venusian sslis, like all other Venusian reptiles, is more highly developed than any Earth lizard.

At last the hungry carnivore spotted his victim. He stopped for a moment, eyeing her, wondering what her flesh would taste like; but he knew that she was not dangerous. She had no claws, no teeth, no protection of any kind. True, she walked upright, as did the blue-green things with the blowguns, but she was obviously not of their species; she was larger, and would provide a better meal.

He moved on, stalking the girl, waiting until she should get to a place where there would be no danger of her falling to the ground below. The sslis did not want to lose this choice morsel to the carrion beetles.

Lanina walked carefully along the intertwining limbs and branches, moving from tree to tree by crawling carefully across the vines that tied one tree to another. And then she realized that she had made a mistake; she had walked out on a great branch which, she presumed, led to the next tree. But it did not; only forty feet out from the mighty trunk of the Empire tree, it came to a dead end. At some time in the past, it had been broken off, perhaps by a lightning bolt, perhaps by internal weakness. Now, it was only a jagged stump.

Realizing that she would have to take another route, she turned to retrace her steps. But the sslis, too, had seen her error, and when she turned, Lanina saw before her the glowing red eyes of the most feared killer on Venus.

In the glowing light of the fluorescent flowers, Lanina could only dimly see the carnivore, but there was no doubt in her mind that it was a killer. It looked something like a terrestrial tiger, but its snout was longer, and it was earless. A ridge of spines ran along its back and down the long, reptilian tail. Slowly, it stalked toward her.

And then, with a terrifying, hissing shriek, it leaped!

WHEN the sslis screamed, Lanina Harrison's mind broke from the paralysis of horror that had seized it, and her hand darted to the ray pistol at her side. With the smooth rapidity of long practice, the weapon came up on a line with the reptile-beast's chest. But Lanina did not fire.

She saw that there was no need to; the beast's chest was already pierced by three long darts from Venusian blowguns. And, even as she watched, a fourth dart leaped from the surrounding leaves and stuck in the rearing animal. The sslis clawed at his chest and screamed again; but the virulent poison on the long darts worked rapidly, and with a final, mortal roar, the great carnivore toppled from the branch and fell crashing through the greenery to the jungle floor far below.

Then silence reigned all through the surrounding jungle. The roars and screams of the dying sslis had silenced the lesser creatures of the forest.

Lanina looked about her, but she could see nothing. There was, however, no doubt in her mind as to what had happened. Kyvor had given orders to the little, blue-green men of the Clan of Tivala to protect her. Even though they chose to remain invisible, she knew they were all about her in the leafy branches. Feeling much safer than she had before, she reholstered her ray pistol and pressed on through the forest.

It was many hours before she reached the spot where the spaceship had crashed into the limbs of the huge Empire tree, and not once was there any evidence that she was being followed by the Tivala.

The spaceship was just as she had left it so many days before; the airlock door was gaping open disclosing the darkness within. She decided to look around inside the ship; there might be some few salvageable things that would materially assist in Wayne's comfort—and her own—during his long convalescence. She had watched Kyvor swing above the dizzying heights from the vines that festooned the Empire trees, and she had no doubt that she could perform the feat equally as well. Her training in the Terran Service had been hard and thorough.

Gingerly, she grasped a nearby vine and pulled, testing her weight upon it. It held. Then she estimated the swing between the limb she was on and the open airlock. She knew that all of this would have taken Kyvor only a fraction of a second to compute, but her Earth-trained responses were too slow for such split-second decisions. One slip meant death.

Sure of herself at last, she clamped her hands tightly about the vine and projected herself out over the green abyss that yawned beneath her. It was a long swing.

Dora Summers heard a scream from the Major's tent and began to run toward it. Then she stopped, frightened, as Major Reeder ran wildly from his tent and across the compound toward the gate.

"Open up!" he screamed. "Open up! Open, I say!"

Dora clasped her hands in front of her mouth as she watched the officer run toward the tank where the gate was. The sentry, accustomed to obeying the orders of his superiors, hastily opened the gate, and the Major ran out into the darkness of the jungle.

Then she started sprinting again, moving rapidly toward the Major's tent. She heard the short, harsh *spit!* of a needle gun just as she neared the entrance to the aluminum-cloth structure. She knew it had not been heard by the others in the camp; the sounds of shouting drowned out the noise of the firing weapon.

Then Captain Bock stepped out of the Major's tent, shouting, "Stop the Major! Stop him! He's gone insane! He's shot the doctor! Stop him!"

As two of the soldiers raced out of the gate to follow the demented commanding officer, Captain Bock turned to look at Lieutenant Summers. The nurse shrank back, frightened. She could tell by the way he looked at her that he suspected that she knew he had killed Captain Ashley.

The doctor had made the mistake of accusing Captain Bock of poisoning Major Reeder. Bock had been in the tent when the Major charged Dr. Ashley; he had, in fact, inflamed the crazed officer's mind against the doctor by telling him that the doctor was attempting to poison him. When Ashley had entered, Captain Bock had grinned sardonically to himself to see his plans working out so well. He had hoped that Major Reeder would actually kill the physician.

But the Major had not; he had merely struck the doctor and run out, his disordered mind unable to function properly. The llomar poison had done its work too well.

The doctor, hardly stunned by the officer's blow had sat up and said, "You did this, Captain! I know you put llomar drug in Major Reeder's food!"

Knowing that the doctor would betray him, the captain's cruel mind could think of only one thing. Accordingly, he drew his needler and shot Ashley before he could say another word. He knew that he could blame the murder on Major Reeder.

He had stepped outside, then, and called to the guard. And then he had turned to see Nurse Summers staring at him. Did she know? Had she guessed that he, and not the Major, had killed Ashley?

"Did you see what Reeder did?" he asked cautiously.

Dora Summers knew that if she betrayed herself the captain would kill her as surely as he had killed Dr. Ashley. Quickly, she shook her head. "I didn't see it. What happened? Is the doctor hurt?"

"Come inside," Bock said. "Take a look. He's dead."

Nurse Summers looked in through the doorway, but she did not go in. Ashley lay there, a small hole burned through his chest by the deadly ray.

By that time, several of the other officers had come out of their quarters, rushing toward the tent of the commanding officer. The entire camp was in an uproar by this time, and Captain Bock had to explain the situation to several of the young subalterns who had come up to him, clamoring for an explanation. He told essentially the same story he had told to Dora. Shortly thereafter, the two sentries who had gone out after the Major returned through the gate and double-timed toward the captain. They came to a halt and saluted.

"We lost him in the jungle, noble sir," said the lance corporal. "He paid no attention to our calls."

"We couldn't follow him into the forest, noble sir," the private explained.

"It is quite obvious that the Major has gone mad," said Captain Bock. "We will wait until dawn and then go on. If he hasn't come back by then, we'll have to assume that he is dead." He paused, and a look of sadness came into his eyes.

"If only there were something we could do for him, poor chap."

"There's nothing, sir," said one of the subalterns. "Once he gets into that jungle, he's a dead man."

"We don't dare go out after him," said another. "We couldn't possibly find him."

Captain Bock looked at the young officer. "We dare not give up hope, Mister Grimes. Organize a patrol, fully armed, and go after him."

The subaltern's eyes opened in surprise, but he said nothing except: "Yes, sir. Right away, sir." Then he turned and strode off.

When the patrol had left, Captain Bock smiled slyly to himself. Whether they returned or not, he knew that they would never find Reeder. Armed only with a needle beam, the Major wouldn't last half an hour in that jungle—if that long.

Then the captain's dark eyes slitted. Dora Summers had gone back to the hospital tent. It was time he had a talk with her. He strode over to the hospital tent and rapped on the door. There was no answer. Then he opened the door and looked inside. She was nowhere to be seen.

Frowning, Captain Bock called to a guard, who came running up subserviently.

"Yes, noble sir?" said the guard.

"Search the compound," Bock said. "Lieutenant Summers is missing. Find her and bring her to me."

The guard saluted. "Yes, noble sir." He turned on his heel and left.

The fact that Dora was missing disturbed the captain. She was necessary to his plans; since the doctor was dead, she would have to be the one to testify that the Major was insane, once the expedition returned to Empire City. Without her assistance, it would be difficult to prove that the Major had been mad before tonight. She could not have left the compound, of course. Only a madman or a fool would go out into the jungle at night. He waited in his tent while the guards searched for the girl, quite confident that she would accede to his wishes. After all, he knew she was a commoner, not a noble. If he threatened her with disclosure to the authorities, she would not only back up his story of Major Reeder's insanity, but would consent to the other plans he had in mind for her. He smiled to himself as he thought of the young nurse's beauty.

CHAPTER SIX

FROM the branches high in the trees above the Imperial Army's bivouac, Kyvor the Killer watched what went on below. When the drug-crazed officer ran out, the jungle-man watched as he ran in a jagged path toward the nearest tree, circled around it, and disappeared beyond the circle of light shed by the illuminating searchlights of the compound. When he had vanished, Kyvor turned his attention back to the four tanks below. He had no further interest in the officer; anyone foolish enough to expose himself to the Venusian jungle unprotected would not live long.

Beside him, Polthan the Hunter chattered softly in the language of the Tivala. "What do we do next, Mighty Fire? The usual gas-pod bombardment?"

Kyvor smiled. "That, yes. But I think I have discovered another method of destroying the invaders. Suppose we were to drop heavy branches into the compound from up here?"

He turned his eyes to watch the scene below while Polthan thought on his chieftain's suggestion. He could hardly see the faces of those who moved beneath him, so high in the

Empire tree was he perched. The tiny figures were like toys that moved mechanically in the panic of the camp.

Meanwhile, Polthan the Hunter thought over what Kyvor had said. Drop heavy branches? What would that do? Could they kill a few of the Earthmen? Yes. But would not most of them flee to the tanks and thus escape death? Most certainly they would. Then what good would it do?

Shaking his frog-like head sadly, Polthan said, "I fear I do not understand your plan, Great Kyvor."

"The carrion beetles," Kyvor said, without looking at the little green man.

A broad smile broke over Polthan's face. The carrion beetles, of course! Who but Kyvor would have thought of such a thing? The carrion beetles which live beneath the mossy covering of the rainforest floor do not come from their burrows unless there are dead things about into which they can chew their way. An ordinary step, even the great weight of a tank tread, would not disturb those it did not crush, but the heavy slam of a falling body told the little creatures that some animal had fallen from the branches overhead—and a sixty-foot fall would kill almost any tree animal. If the thing did not move, the beetles would crawl from their holes to attack it.

Polthan's broad mouth smiled as he thought of the confusion that would result in the Earthmen's camp.

"I will find the branch, Polthan," Kyvor said. "You run and find some gas pods. Quickly, now."

Without bothering to answer, Polthan scurried off through the trees.

Kyvor, intent on finding a branch of the proper size to simulate a falling body, did not see, in the camp far below, a girl in a white uniform climb over the body of one of the great tanks and disappear into the jungle. She glanced behind her and ran.

Polthan the Hunter ranged far into the upper terrace of the Venusian jungle searching for the brittle pods of the gas vine. He headed toward one area where he knew the pods would be, a spot high in the trees above where the Earthly spaceship had smashed into the forest. As he neared the spot, his sensitive ears heard the low conversation of his people, so he changed course slightly and within a few moments found the little group surrounding the spaceship.

Mylthat the Trapper and Volthys the Scout were standing on a nearby branch as Polthan swung down from above.

"What are you doing?" Polthan wanted to know.

"The female of Earth left the tree-cavern where Kyvor the Chieftain left her," Mylthat explained. "We were told to watch over her, and we have done so. She has just gone into the sky-vessel. Where is Mighty Kyvor and what is he doing?"

"We followed the Empire Army's trail as they moved along in their great machines, and they are now camped less than an hour's walk from here. Kyvor has decided to harass them with carrion beetles and then drop gas pods upon them. He has sent me to gather the pods." His frog-like face broke into a grin as he said, "One of the Earthmen is already accounted for. He went mad and rushed into the jungle. Be not surprised if you hear his death cry in the forest."

Volthys the Scout nodded sagely. "It is well. Should we help you gather the gas pods, Polthan?"

Polthan frowned in concentration. Finally, he said, "The great Kyvor ordered that the female be protected, but he did not say how many were to protect her. If some of you come with me to gather gas pods, and some of you stay here to watch the female, we can do the work well, and do it as Mighty Kyvor has ordered."

Volthys nodded. "So be it. Come; I will bring others and we will hunt for pods. Mylthat can stay and watch the she."

"So be it," agreed Mylthat. Thus it was that the Clan of Tivala swung off through the trees to search for gas pods, leaving the sturdy Mylthat to protect Lanina. He sat on the monstrous branch gazing quietly at the blackness of the open airlock, awaiting the reappearance of the girl, little knowing what was taking place within the hull of the broken ship.

Dora Summers knew that her life was not worth a snap of the fingers if Captain Bock ever discovered that she knew that he had been the one to kill Dr. Ashley. Her only way out was to flee to the jungle. The thought frightened her, of course; she had heard of the deadliness of the Venusian rain forest. But she had seen no evidence of its deadliness during the expedition. Not once had they been attacked by any of the denizens of the surrounding jungle.

How she would survive, she had no notion; but she nevertheless knew that her chances would be far better in the forest than they would be with Captain Bock. Now that he was commander of the expedition, he could easily have her killed without calling suspicion on himself. Nurse Summers much preferred the mercies of nature to the mercilessness of Captain Bock.

Thus it was that within a few moments after she left the officer, she had gathered together a few supplies and a blaster rifle and, watching her chance, had climbed over one of the tanks and escaped into the forest.

It was not until she had left the circle of light that illuminated the campsite that she realized the beauty of the rain forest surrounding her. The glowing light from the vine blossoms gave her a dim illumination that was quite sufficient for her to see her way through the forest. Holding her blaster rifle at the ready, she walked onward through the jungle.

Around her rose the great Empire trees, mighty, aloof giants that towered into the glowing haze above her. Beneath her feet, the thick moss of the jungle floor gave slightly, as though she were walking across a gigantic featherbed. Around her, she could hear the normal noises of the jungle night; whisperings, grunts, and distant screams and roars that made her uneasy with dread.

Several times, she heard the rustle of moving animals near her and pressed herself against the thick, rough bark of a nearby tree. It was only at these times that she realized the true vastness of the comforting Empire trees. The thought that they were the greatest living things in the Solar System, and that, in spite of their vastness and impersonal majesty, they seemed somehow friendly, was of great comfort to her.

As the long Venusian night passed, Dora Summers became more and more weary. Finally, tired and exhausted from her long march, she sought some place where she could safely sleep. At long last, she discovered a dark pit in the thick, heavy bark of one of the gigantic trees and, taking her flashlight from her belt, pointed it at the hole. It was twenty feet off the ground, and the only way she could reach it was to climb the trunk of the tree. Shutting off her light, she grasped the projections of the thick bark and began to climb upwards.

It was like climbing a wall. The Empire tree was a thousand feet thick, and nearly a mile in circumference; up close, it was hard to see that the trunk curved gradually; it looked like a huge, rough wooden wall. When she reached the hole, she held her rifle in one hand while she aimed the flashlight with the other. The hole was empty.

She went in, and leaned back against the rear wall of the tree-cavern, holding her rifle in her lap. For a long time, she could not sleep, but at last drowsiness stole over her. Overcome with fatigue she slept hard.

She did not know how many hours she slept, but she was awakened by a slight sound, and her eyes opened quickly in fear. At first, she could see nothing but a vague shadow. It had grown light outside, and the figure of the intruder was looming large between her and the entrance to the tree-cavern. Instinctively, she clutched for the blaster rifle that she had held in her lap. It was gone!

And then she recognized what it was that had invaded her tree-cavern.

Standing over her, the blaster-rifle in his hands, was Major Lyman Reeder, who had been driven insane by the llomar drug!

CHAPTER SEVEN

KYVOR THE KILLER waited patiently for Polthan to return. Time meant nothing to Kyvor; in the jungle there was no need of rushing to meet a time schedule, as more "civilized" men did. There was plenty of time to attack the Imperial Army bivouac below. Therefore, Kyvor amused himself by watching what went on in the camp. He had lowered himself to a long branch that projected over the tent of the commanding officer, and then, hiding himself in the thick leaves of a vine, had climbed down to within a few feet of the aluminum-cloth shelter.

Long he hung there silently, listening to the conversations that took place beneath him and watching what went on in the camp. When the detail that had been assigned to search for Major Reeder returned, Kyvor smiled grimly as he heard the subaltern's report.

The young subaltern saluted Captain Bock and said, "Sir, we have searched the area thoroughly. Major Reeder's footprints can't be traced. The moss soon springs back and covers every trace."

Captain Bock was agitated. "I see," he said. "Did you find any other footprints? Lieutenant Dora Summers has been missing for some hours."

The subaltern shook his head. "No, sir. We found no traces of anyone else in the jungle. What happened, if I may ask, sir?"

"She disappeared," said the captain. "I'm wondering if some jungle beast may not have gotten her. I ordered that the camp be searched, but we could find no trace of her. I hardly think that she would have left of her own accord."

Within his scheming mind, Captain Bock actually did not understand why the nurse was missing. For Nurse Summers had made a mistake; she had not realized that she had fooled Captain Bock completely; she had not realized that the officer did not believe that she knew he had killed Captain Ashley.

"How could any beast get inside the compound, sir?" the subaltern asked.

"I don't know," Bock answered, "but I've ordered the guard doubled. We can't afford to be hampered now; the technicians have located the Earth spaceship. According to their detectors, the vessel is within a few miles of here. It seems to have landed in the branches of one of the trees, because the detectors point to a spot several hundred feet in the air. Therefore, we will move toward it at dawn tomorrow."

The subaltern saluted. "Very well, sir. Shall we prepare now to move?"

Captain Bock nodded. "Get the men ready. We will want to start the tanks as soon as the sun comes up. It's hard to see anything under the darkness of the clouds, but at least the sun supplies some light."

The subaltern turned on his heel and left.

Fifteen minutes later, the temporary camp was full of soldiers moving about, attempting to get everything ready for the morning's march. It was at that point that the turmoil began.

From some place in the trees high above them, a broken branch came hurtling down. It crashed to the ground in the center of the camp, but did not hit anyone. For several seconds, no one paid any attention; then, suddenly, the mossy ground beneath the soldiers seemed to come alive. From all over, little creatures the size of a man's thumb crawled out of their burrows and headed blindly for the broken branch that had fallen with such force on the turf beneath. When their gnashing mandibles found a soldier's boot, they began to chew, and the Imperial Expeditionary force found themselves beating off the little things everywhere. Then, without warning, something popped in the middle of the camp, and a cloud of acrid, smoky vapor arose from it. Soon, others were falling and popping, filling the air with the poisonous gas. Men began to choke and cough as the fumes entered their lungs, and in the space of a few seconds, the camp was transformed from an orderly military bivouac to a chaotic, milling crowd of men.

In the branches of the trees high above the Imperial Army, Kyvor was directing the placement of the gas bombs. The pods were filled with a gas, which was released when the brittle shells cracked as they struck the ground below.

At last, Kyvor whistled shrilly, and the aerial bombardment ceased. The soldiers in the encampment were all lying on the moss. There was no movement anywhere in the camp.

"Come," Kyvor called to the Clan of Tivala. "We have more work. The Earthmen will bother us no more."

Volthys the Scout picked that moment to run up to Kyvor.

"Mighty Kyvor!" he said breathlessly. "You must come! I saw her! I saw the Good Lady!"

Kyvor stood up from where he had been squatting on a branch and grasped the little blue-green Venusian by the throat. "Do not say such things! I do not like that kind of joke, Volthys!"

"I do not joke, Great Kyvor," the little man chattered. "I do not lie! I saw her! Believe me, I saw her! It was the Good Lady! She is not far away; come! I will show you!"

Kyvor's broad brow frowned in thought. The Scout did not lie; that much, Kyvor knew. But he must be mistaken. Still—

Kyvor decided quickly. If there were anyone left in the Imperial Camp, they could be taken care of later. Right now, this new mystery had to be explored. Calling to the Clan of Tivala to follow him, Kyvor the Killer began swinging through the trees toward the spot where Volthys the Hunter had claimed to see the Good Lady.

Once inside the airlock of the spaceship, Lanina tied the vine to a nearby stanchion. She had no intention of allowing the thing to swing back and maroon her in the ship again. She did not see the sinuous form of a tree snake glide silently down the vine after she had secured her end of it—and neither did Mylthat the Trapper, who was, at that moment watching his clansmen swing off into the trees in search of gas pods. When he again returned his attention to the open airlock, all was normal.

Lanina walked into the spaceship, shining her light before her. As she entered the control room, she heard a faint humming noise. Sweeping her beam around the room, she saw almost immediately what it was. One of the instruments on the control panel was still operating; evidently at least part of the power was still on. A red light glowed in one section of the panel. Since she was walking along what was actually one wall of the control room, she did not immediately see what instrument was calling for attention. The control panel was now running up and down instead of from left to right. Then, as she neared the glittering crimson globe, she saw what it was. Someone was using a detector on the ship!

Carefully, she checked the instrument readings. Whoever had located the ship was using a detector less than two miles to the northeast. That would be the Imperial Army! And that would be where Kyvor was.

Unhesitatingly, she turned and walked back toward the airlock. Just as she was about to step up to the port itself, something hissed venomously and a long neck rose up between her and the door. This time, Lanina was not caught napping. Her hand flashed to the holster at her hip and brought out the ray pistol in a single smooth motion. Her finger touched the trigger for the briefest instant.

The tree-snake's triumphant victory hiss was cut short as the ray beam burned his head off, leaving nothing but a headless, writhing corpse that thrashed like a great whip as death gripped it.

Lanina waited until the snake's convulsions had ceased, and then she stepped over the sinuous body to the airlock door. Her vine was gone. As he had crawled down it to attack the girl, the tree snake had loosened it from where the girl had looped it around a stanchion, and it had swung free again. Unless she could get another vine, she would be stranded in the spaceship again.

She was not afraid, however; the little, blue-green men outside would push a vine over to her, if she could only make them understand what it was that she wanted.

She did not realize that only one member of the Clan was left outside. And Mylthat the Trapper could not help her; he was unconscious. The ray beam that had blasted off the head of the tree snake had narrowly missed Mylthat, who had been standing on a branch outside the airlock. The searing energy of the ray had sizzled viciously past his head, burning the skin, and dropping him where he stood.

Fortunately, he had not fallen off the huge branch, but he was of no use to Lanina. Leaning precariously out of the airlock door, Lanina struggled to attract the attention of Mylthat.

CHAPTER EIGHT

CAPTAIN BOCK lifted himself dizzily to his feet. He shook his head, trying to clear it. What had happened? He put his hand to his face and felt something covering it. Slowly, his memory began to come back.

Something had started popping outside his tent, and he had smelled gas. He had had just enough time to get a gas mask out of the emergency locker when unconsciousness overtook him.

Grasping for the wall, the officer lurched toward the door. He leaned against the doorjamb and gazed out at a scene of carnage. Sprawled all around him lay unmoving men, crumpled in ungainly attitudes on the moss. Nothing moved anywhere.

How long had he been unconscious? Captain Bock looked at his watch and then at the sky. He could not actually see the sky itself, for the leafy branches of the mighty Empire trees screened the ground from the pearly light of the ever-clouded sky, but he could see that the night had gone and day had come.

He could reconstruct what had happened; he had not had enough of the gas to kill him, and his gas mask had protected him while he lay in a stupor on the floor of his tent. But where had the gas come from? He waited until he could stand up again; then, when his strength had returned, he walked out into the clearing. He almost immediately caught sight of fragments of what looked like thin pieces of wood. He picked one up, and the shard broke between his fingers like broken glass.

Frowning behind the thick goggles of the gas mask, the captain thought over what had happened and tried to link it with something he remembered reading about, years before. Then it came to him. Here and there in the jungle grew a vine that had a peculiar way of protecting its seeds. The seeds grew in pods, which were filled with a gas that was generated by the plant. Thus, when the seedpods fell, they cracked open and filled the air surrounding them with a poisonous vapor. This vapor killed the insects in the moss, which might otherwise eat the seed before it could begin to sprout and grow. Somehow, a great many of these pods had been dropped on the camp from the trees above.

Suddenly, Captain Bock realized that he was alone in the jungles of Venus! Alone! Without the armed might of his men behind him, the captain began to tremble in fear as he looked at the jungle around him. A moss-eating lizard appeared several yards away and looked at the captain through the strong fence that stretched between two of the tanks. The officer did not know it was harmless; he grabbed a rifle that had fallen from one of the soldier's hands and fired at the animal. So shaky was his aim, however, that the deadly ray missed and the frightened moss-eater bounded into the protection of the jungle.

Captain Bock felt cold perspiration form on his brow. He had to get back to Empire City! Gone were any thoughts of returning in glory at the head of a successful expedition; his only thoughts now were to escape the terrifying jungle. Quickly, he ran to the nearest tank and climbed inside. He started the motor and threw the tank in gear. Twisting the controls, he headed the tank back the way the expedition had come.

Or, he thought he did. Actually, his sense of direction had become distorted by fear, and he was heading almost directly away from his goal.

For several minutes, he drove the tank at full speed, as though he were pursued by all the monsters of the Venusian rain forest. He was only brought to a halt when something extraordinary happened ahead of him. He saw something fall from the air above and land on the mossy floor of the jungle. He brought the tank to a full stop when he saw it was a lovely young, blond-haired girl. The carrion beetles were already coming out of their burrows when Captain Bock jumped out of the tank and ran out to get her. He reached her first.

Now that his fear had cooled somewhat, the Imperial officer's shrewd, calculating mind was working again. He knew that the girl could only be one of the people who had come in the Earth ship. If he could bring her back as a prisoner, with a story of how he had captured her himself after the entire expedition had been wiped out to a man, he would be even more of a hero—

The carrion beetles scattered at his approach, for, in spite of their vicious jaws, they will not attack anything that is living and moving. Some few took a snap at his boots and began to chew, but they did not hang on long.

The captain lifted the girl up and took her to the tank. He put her in a seat in the rear, tied her up, and started the tank moving again.

As he moved through the trees, Kyvor said softly to the little green man beside him, "Volthys, if you are lying, I shall cut out your tongue and feed it to the bat-lizards!"

"I do not lie!" Volthys chattered in protest. "The mighty Kyvor knows I do not lie! She was near this spot. I saw her and ran to tell you. I—"

He stopped then, because the hissing scream of a maddened sslis echoed through the leafy jungle.

"Hush!" said Kyvor. "Something is wrong here! The sslis is below us!"

"Aye," said Polthan from a nearby branch. "And the sslis does not hunt on the ground."

"Come!" Kyvor shouted and swung quickly in the direction from which the sound had come. If there were a strange girl in the jungle, it would only be she who was being attacked by the reptilian carnivore. No other prey of the sslis would be on the ground.

But, as he approached, Kyvor saw it was not a girl. Instead, a single man was standing, his back against a tree, a long stick in his hand. In front of him snarled the huge sslis. Each time the reptile lunged, the stick struck out to meet it, striking the savage snout and causing the beast-lizard to retreat.

Kyvor watched for several minutes, and his admiration for the man below began to grow. Never had he seen a so-called civilized man display such courage and skill in the face of certain death. Unarmed and nearly naked though he was, the man nevertheless seemed determined to live in spite of the odds against him. But he was not a young man, there were traces of gray in the hair at his temples, and his body showed that, although it had once been that of an athlete, it was not in fine trim. Gradually, the man began to weaken, and the carnivore's lunges came closer and closer.

Kyvor made his decision. No man, no matter who he was, deserved to die when he could display such bravery in the face of death.

Kyvor the Killer grasped a long vine and launched himself through the air toward the snarling beast-lizard below. Just as the great sslis lifted himself for a final, fatal attack on the beleaguered man, Kyvor's mighty body struck him, bowling him over from the force of the blow.

Kyvor locked his legs about the beast's abdomen and curled one powerful arm around the tough, leathery throat. There had been no time to pull the long knife from the scabbard at his waist, and the twisting and rolling of the sslis did not permit him to do so, even now. Over and over the reptile rolled, trying to dislodge the man-thing from its back.

But Kyvor knew that to be shaken off meant death. Grimly he hung on, fighting to get one arm locked around the back of the beast-lizard's neck. At last, he held the sslis's head in a hammerlock. Back and back he forced the head, while the reptile roared and hissed in rage and pain. Kyvor's powerful muscles tensed more and more, increasing the pressure. Suddenly, there issued from the throat of the carnivore a horrendous scream—then there was a loud *crack!* and the animal fell, unmoving, to the moss, its neck broken.

Kyvor pushed the great body off himself, and as he stood up, the man who had been beating off the reptile with a stick walked over to him, his hand outstretched.

"Sir," said the stranger, "I do not know who you are, but you have saved my life. That was the most magnificent piece of work I have ever had the honor to see. Whatever you may ask of me, I will gladly risk my life to do it, as you have risked yours for me."

Kyvor accepted the outstretched hand and found that the grip was firm and friendly. The gray eyes that looked steadily into Kyvor's own reflected the intelligence of the brain behind them.

"Your own defense was a measure of your courage," the fire-haired giant said. "I am called Kyvor. And you?"

The man drew himself up proudly. "Major Lyman Reeder, of his Imperial Majesty's army, at your service, sir."

No surprise registered on Kyvor's face; he had known that the man must be one of the Imperial soldiers, although he had not realized that it was the commanding officer of the expedition. It might, perhaps, have been better to allow the man to die at the mercy of the sslis, but Kyvor would never have done that. Courage should always be rewarded with courage.

Before Kyvor said anything, Volthys the Scout dropped down from the trees, sliding down a thick vine.

"I found her, Mighty Kyvor," he said excitedly. "I found the Good Lady. She's asleep in a tree-cavern not far from here. She's all dressed in white, though, and she wears the insignia of the Empire, which the Good Lady would never wear."

Kyvor's eyes narrowed in thought, and he turned to look at the Major. That officer had drawn back at the appearance of the green man, and held his stick again at the ready, in case of attack. The flame-haired giant, ignoring the Major's stance, said, "Do you happen to know a young woman with black hair and brown eyes who would be wearing the uniform of a nurse in the Imperial Army?"

The Major nodded. "That would be Lieutenant Dora Summers. Why?"

"She's in a tree-cavern near here. What would she be doing out in the jungle, away from your camp?"

Major Reeder shook his head. "I don't know. You see, I—I've been ill. I don't know what happened. I can only remember very dimly that I ran away from my men and—and I ran into the jungle and tore my clothes off. I only came out of it a short time ago, but since then, my brain seems to be clearer than ever before. Frankly, I do not understand it."

"Nor do I," Kyvor said. "However that may be, I would like to talk to that girl. I wonder if it wouldn't be better if you woke her up; seeing me or my friends might shock her."

Major Reeder nodded in agreement. "Whatever you say, Kyvor. Where is the girl?"

The jungle-man spoke to the green Venusian, and the little man pointed toward a tree some distance away, while chattering in a tongue unfamiliar to the Imperial officer.

Kyvor turned back to the Major and said, "Come; I'll show you."

They walked toward the great tree, and as they approached it, Kyvor pointed toward a dark scar about twenty feet off the ground. "She's in there," he said. "Can you climb up?"

"I'm sure I can," Major Reeder replied.

CHAPTER NINE

WHEN Dora Summers awoke, she realized instantly that the man standing over her was not the same Major Reeder that she had known before, and when he spoke, she was sure of it.

"How are you, Lieutenant?" he asked in a kindly voice. "I picked up the blaster rifle because I was afraid you might shoot before you saw who I was. Or, perhaps—" He smiled. "—perhaps even after, considering the way I've treated you in the past."

"You recovered from the llomar drug!" the girl said. "Why, that's wonderful! Then you've—" She broke off as another figure appeared in the entrance to the tree-cavern, a tall, golden-skinned, flame-haired young man who stopped and looked at her for a long moment without saying anything.

"Who—who is this?" the nurse asked.

"He calls himself Kyvor," the Major explained. "He risked his life to save mine; I am eternally indebted to him."

"You were about to say something about the llomar drug," Kyvor said. "What was it?"

"Captain Bock stole some of the drug from the medical supplies," the girl explained. "He gave an overdose to the Major in order to drive him insane and kill him. The captain wanted to take command of the expedition, so that he would get all the credit when we returned to Empire City.

"Llomar usually kills when given in an overdose. But in about one case out of a thousand, the insanity wears off after a few hours, and the patient becomes more sane than he ever was before in his life. No one knows for sure how it works."

"I see," Major Reeder said softly. "That explains why I understand many things more clearly now. I can see the pettiness and small-mindedness of the Imperial Court; I can understand the fear and stupidity that hangs over the city like the clouds. And I can see the insanity and cruelty of the whole system of government." He closed his eyes. "I can't go back there; I have no place in such a society any longer."

Kyvor looked at the man for a long time before he said anything. He was judging and weighing the man's character. At long last, he said, "Sit down, both of you. There are some things you should know." He looked first at the girl. "You are Dora Summers, you say. Isn't your real name Dora Larsen?"

The girl's hand flew to her mouth in astonishment. "How did you know?"

"Your father's name was Edmond Larsen," Kyvor continued. "He was executed ten years ago for treasonal utterances against the Emperor. Your mother married Colonel

Summers of the Imperial Army, giving him a false story and background. She didn't want anyone to know you were a commoner. Summers accepted her story and gave you his name, but you've been afraid ever since that someone would find it out."

"How do you know all this?" the girl repeated.

"Your father was my uncle," Kyvor said. "My mother was Elaine Larsen. You look a great deal like her; that's why I was so surprised when I first saw you. My friends, the Tivala, thought you *were* my mother, whom they called the Good Lady. They are simple folk, and believe the evidence of their senses rather than their memories; they thought you were Elaine Larsen, even though she has been dead for thirteen years."

Major Reeder had been watching the nurse while Kyvor spoke, and when the golden giant had finished, the Major put his hand on the girl's shoulder. "Don't worry about me, my dear. Your secret is safe with me."

"I am sure of it," Kyvor said. "Else I would not have told her in your presence; I trust you, Major, but before I tell you anything more, I must ask you a question.

"You said that you could see the corruption of the Empire, where you were blind to it before. Major, how would you like to help bring the Empire down around the ears of Derek the Second?"

There was silence in the tree-cavern for a long time. The Major gazed out at the jungle, his mind in deep thought. Neither the jungle-man nor the nurse spoke, not wanting to break the Major's introspection.

Finally the Major looked at Kyvor, and his gray eyes were calm. "I gave my oath to uphold the Emperor," he said. "And for no other man would I break that oath, even though I felt it to be in error. But I owe you a debt I can never repay, Kyvor; and besides, I have a feeling that you may succeed. I'll help you. What are your plans?"

"My name, the name my parents gave me, is Glen Neilson. Perhaps you have heard of Dr. Simon Neilson? He was my father," Kyvor began. He went on to explain that two Earth agents had landed and had plans for contacting Earth. With aid inside Empire City, it would be possible to destroy the Empire and liberate the enslaved commoners.

"But how can I help?" the Major asked when Kyvor was through.

"It will be simple, Major. Your camp was gassed last night; my friends and I attacked it. Usually, we tear down the fences afterwards and leave the men to the wild beasts. But we did not do so this time because we were told that the girl—Dora, here—was in the jungle. The gas does not kill; it merely puts men into a deep sleep. With the protection of the fence and tanks around them, they will be safe. Most of them are probably awake by now.

"All you have to do is take command again, arrest this Captain Bock, and then lead them to where the spaceship is. You, yourself, can inspect it. You can then report that no one lived through the crash, that the occupants have probably been eaten by wild beasts.

"Then you will simply go back to Empire City and resume your old way of life until I contact you again."

"I see," said Major Reeder. "Very well; it sounds like a good plan to me. I'll do it." Then he looked at the nurse. "I'll tell them that you came after me when the captain poisoned me. That will account for your absence."

Dora Summers nodded and smiled. "We'd better get started, though," she cautioned. "Captain Bock may be up to even more of his nefarious schemes."

Kyvor rose to his feet. "Come," he said.

As they neared the spot where the encampment was, they heard the sound of blaster fire, and the Major broke into a run. Kyvor took to the trees, in order to travel faster. He could move through the lower terrace of the rain forest much more rapidly than a man could walk along the mossy floor.

When he finally came to the camp, he was surprised by what he saw. One of the tanks had been driven off, leaving a hole in the defenses of the compound. Several of the soldiers were firing at a group of animals that had wandered into the area. None of the animals were dangerous, but the soldiers were not familiar with the jungle fauna, and so could not tell the claws of the moss-diggers from the claws of a carnivore.

It was at that moment that Mylthat the Trapper scurried up to Kyvor's side. There was a nasty burn along one side of his head.

"Mighty Kyvor," he gasped. "I have been searching for you for hours, it seems."

"What is it, Mylthat?" the jungle-man asked.

Mylthat explained about the golden-haired she. He told how the girl had gone to the spaceship and how he had happened to get the burn on his head.

"—and then, Mighty Fire-Hair, I awoke just as she became desperate. The vine was only a few feet out of her reach, so she jumped for it. But it gave a little, and, as she slid down, it gave more. She slid down the vine for over a hundred feet before it finally tore loose and dropped her to the ground. I could do nothing for her; I was too dizzy from the hurt of the death-gun.

"As she lay there, one of the rumbling machines of the Empire men stopped, and a man got out and put her inside. Then the machine went away."

At the thought of the beautiful, blonde Lanina in the hands of the murderous Captain Bock, a low growl came from Kyvor's throat. He would have been well content to allow the officer to die by himself in the jungle, but this was a different matter.

Without another word, he leaped to his feet and grasped a vine. Then he vanished in a long, swinging arc.

CHAPTER TEN

As MAJOR REEDER ran up to the camp, a young subaltern ran out to meet him.

"Sir!" he said, "are you all right? Something happened during the night. We were gassed and when we awoke, we found that someone had taken a tank, and Captain Bock was missing."

"It was the captain who took the tank," Reeder said coldly. "He has proven himself not only a traitor, but a thief. It was he who drugged my coffee and made me seem insane."

"And it was he who murdered Captain Ashley," Nurse Summers said. "I was just outside his tent when he did it."

"Mister Grimes," the Major addressed the subaltern, "get the men organized quickly. We must go to the Earth spaceship and investigate, then take our report back to the Emperor.

"I hardly think we need worry about Captain Bock. If he survives, he can only go to Empire City, where he will immediately be arrested as a traitor and a murderer. If he does not survive—" Major Reeder shrugged. "Justice will be served in either case."

The subaltern saluted. "Very well, sir. We'll be ready to go very soon."

High in the upper terraces of the Venusian rain forest, moving with the utmost speed of which he was capable, Kyvor raced after the retreating tank. He moved alone; at top speed, he outdistanced even the quick-moving Polthan. No

Venusian could hope to keep up with the flame-haired giant if Kyvor chose to outpace his green-skinned friends.

Occasionally, he dropped to the lower branches to check the trail of the moving tank; human footprints faded rapidly in the springy moss of the jungle floor, but the treads of a heavy tank were more permanent. His keen eyes needed only the merest hint to follow a trail, and, as he moved onward, the trail became fresher and clearer—he was gaining!

Lanina felt a rough hand shaking her.

"Wake up!" said a harsh voice. "Come! Wake up!"

She shook the sleep from her weary brain and sat up in the cramped seat of the tank. Captain Bock was glaring at her from the front seat. "Wake up!" he repeated.

Lanina looked at him coldly without saying anything. She wriggled a little, trying to make herself more comfortable; for two days, her hands had been locked together by magnetic handcuffs, twisting her arms cruelly behind her back, but not once had she given any indication of discomfort to her captor.

Captain Bock looked untidy and unkempt; his beard bristled through an ugly coating of dust, grease, and perspiration, which did nothing to improve his foul disposition.

"Get out," he said sharply. "Something's happened to the tank. The motor refuses to turn over. We'll have to fix it."

Lanina shrugged her shoulders contemptuously. "How am I to help you with handcuffs around my wrists!"

He grasped her roughly by the shoulder. "Don't argue! When I get you back to Empire City, I'll show you that you can't argue with an Imperial officer! If it weren't for the fact that the Emperor would punish me if I didn't bring you in perfect condition, I'd—"

"I'm sure you would," Lanina cut in. "You're not a man; you're a beast."

Bock snarled and lashed out with his open palm. There was a sharp crack. Lanina's cheek flamed red from the sting of the cowardly blow.

"Now get out!" he shouted. "We have work to do!"

Wordlessly, Lanina obeyed. What else could she do? If she refused, she knew full well that the sadistic captain would beat her into insensibility. She had been with him in the tank for two days, and she knew how his twisted mind worked.

When they were both outside of the vehicle, the officer unlocked the engine compartment of the tank, disclosing the turboelectric motor that lay within. After several minutes of inspection, he said, "The injector valves have become fouled. We'll have to change them."

"If you think I'm going to help you," Lanina said in an icy voice, "you're insane."

Again he turned on her, fury burning in his hate-filled eyes. Mouthing foul oaths, he slapped her again and again, forehand and backhand, until her senses began to reel. She fell to the mossy ground, and he stood over her, glaring down. He started to say more, but, quite suddenly, he glanced up, as though he had seen something out of the corner of his eye. He looked up, and an expression of terror crossed his face.

His hand moved toward his holster, but he was too slow and too late. The huge form of a giant sslis leaped upon him from the branches of a nearby tree. With a terrified scream, Captain Bock tried to turn and run. The sslis missed its target by a few feet, clawing the captain's arm. In a panic of fear, the Imperial officer turned and ran toward the jungle. The sslis snarled viciously and bounded after the fleeing craven.

At that moment, Kyvor the Killer was only a quarter of a mile away. He heard the hunting cry of the sslis, and knowing that he was very close to the tank he had been following for so long, he redoubled his efforts, increasing his speed through the jungle.

At last, he came upon the clearing where the tank had stalled. There, just outside the open door, lay the unconscious figure of Lanina.

Within seconds, Kyvor had dropped to the ground, and had clasped the girl in his arms. "Lanina! Lanina! What's happened?"

Groggily, she opened her eyes. When she saw the bronzed giant who was holding her, she smiled and threw her arms about him. Then, suddenly she pushed him away. "I'm sorry," she said. "I forgot that you belong to another."

"Another?" Kyvor frowned. "What are you talking about?"

"Don't pretend," she said. "I saw the photograph of the dark-haired girl in your tree-cave."

For a moment, Kyvor's frown persisted, then a smile broke over his face. "Good heaven, girl! That picture is twenty years old! That's my mother!"

A sudden joyous light burst into the girl's eyes as her arms clasped him again.

In the distance, they could hear the satisfied grunts of the sslis as it fed gruesomely on its human prey. Captain Bock would never be a menace to anyone again.

THE END

If you've enjoyed this book, you will not want to miss these terrific titles…

ARMCHAIR SCI-FI & HORROR DOUBLE NOVELS, $12.95 each

D-61 **THE MAN WHO STOPPED AT NOTHING** by Paul W. Fairman
TEN FROM INFINITY by Ivar Jorgensen

D-62 **WORLDS WITHIN** by Rog Phillips
THE SLAVE by C.M. Kornbluth

D-63 **SECRET OF THE BLACK PLANET** by Milton Lesser
THE OUTCASTS OF SOLAR III by Emmett McDowell

D-64 **WEB OF THE WORLDS** by Harry Harrison and Katherine MacLean
RULE GOLDEN by Damon Knight

D-65 **TEN TO THE STARS** by Raymond Z. Gallun
THE CONQUERORS by David H. Keller, M. D.

D-66 **THE HORDE FROM INFINITY** by Dwight V. Swain
THE DAY THE EARTH FROZE by Gerald Hatch

D-67 **THE WAR OF THE WORLDS** by H. G. Wells
THE TIME MACHINE by H. G. Wells

D-68 **STARCOMBERS** by Edmond Hamilton
THE YEAR WHEN STARDUST FELL by Raymond F. Jones

D-69 **HOCUS-POCUS UNIVERSE** by Jack Williamson
QUEEN OF THE PANTHER WORLD by Berkeley Livingston

D-70 **BATTERING RAMS OF SPACE** by Don Wilcox
DOOMSDAY WING by George H. Smith

ARMCHAIR SCIENCE FICTION & FANTASY CLASSICS, $12.95 each

C-19 **EMPIRE OF JEGGA**
by David V. Reed

C-20 **THE TOMORROW PEOPLE**
by Judith Merril

C-21 **THE MAN FROM YESTERDAY**
by Howard Browne as by Lee Francis

C-22 **THE TIME TRADERS**
by Andre Norton

C-23 **ISLANDS OF SPACE**
by John W. Campbell

C-24 **THE GALAXY PRIMES**
by E. E. "Doc" Smith

If you've enjoyed this book, you will not want to miss these terrific titles…

ARMCHAIR SCI-FI & HORROR DOUBLE NOVELS, $12.95 each

D-71   **THE DEEP END** by Gregory Luce
          TO WATCH BY NIGHT by Robert Moore Williams

D-72   **SWORDSMAN OF LOST TERRA** by Poul Anderson
          PLANET OF GHOSTS by David V. Reed

D-73   **MOON OF BATTLE** by J. J. Allerton
          THE MUTANT WEAPON by Murray Leinster

D-74   **OLD SPACEMEN NEVER DIE!** John Jakes
          RETURN TO EARTH by Bryan Berry

D-75   **THE THING FROM UNDERNEATH** by Milton Lesser
          OPERATION INTERSTELLAR by George O. Smith

D-76   **THE BURNING WORLD** by Algis Budrys
          FOREVER IS TOO LONG by Chester S. Geier

D-77   **THE COSMIC JUNKMAN** by Rog Phillips
          THE ULTIMATE WEAPON by John W. Campbell

D-78   **THE TIES OF EARTH** by James H. Schmitz
          CUE FOR QUIET by Thomas L. Sherred

D-79   **SECRET OF THE MARTIANS** by Paul W. Fairman
          THE VARIABLE MAN by Philip K. Dick

D-80   **THE GREEN GIRL** by Jack Williamson
          THE ROBOT PERIL by Don Wilcox

ARMCHAIR SCIENCE FICTION CLASSICS, $12.95 each

C-25   **THE STAR KINGS**
  b   y Edmond Hamilton

C-26   **NOT IN SOLITUDE**
          by Kenneth Gantz

C-32   **PROMETHEUS II**
          by S. J. Byrne

ARMCHAIR SCIENCE FICTION & HORROR GEMS SERIES, $12.95 each

G-7   **SCIENCE FICTION GEMS, Vol. Seven**
          Jack Sharkey and others

G-8   **HORROR GEMS, Vol. Eight**
          Seabury Quinn and others

If you've enjoyed this book, you will not want to miss these terrific titles...

ARMCHAIR SCI-FI, FANTASY, & HORROR DOUBLE NOVELS, $12.95 each

D-81 **THE LAST PLEA** by Robert Bloch
THE STATUS CIVILIZATION by Robert Sheckley

D-82 **WOMAN FROM ANOTHER PLANET** by Frank Belknap Long
HOMECALLING by Judith Merril

D-83 **WHEN TWO WORLDS MEET** by Robert Moore Williams
THE MAN WHO HAD NO BRAINS by Jeff Sutton

D-84 **THE SPECTRE OF SUICIDE SWAMP** by E. K. Jarvis
IT'S MAGIC, YOU DOPE! by Jack Sharkey

D-85 **THE STARSHIP FROM SIRIUS** by Rog Phillips
FINAL WEAPON by Everett Cole

D-86 **TREASURE ON THUNDER MOON** by Edmond Hamilton
TRAIL OF THE ASTROGAR by Henry Haase

D-87 **THE VENUS ENIGMA** by Joe Gibson
THE WOMAN IN SKIN 13 by Paul W. Fairman

D-88 **THE MAD ROBOT** by William P. McGivern
THE RUNNING MAN by J. Holly Hunter

D-89 **VENGEANCE OF KYVOR** by Randall Garrett
AT THE EARTH'S CORE by Edgar Rice Burroughs

D-90 **DWELLERS OF THE DEEP** by Don Wilcox
NIGHT OF THE LONG KNIVES by Fritz Leiber

ARMCHAIR SCIENCE FICTION CLASSICS, $12.95 each

C-28 **THE MAN FROM TOMORROW**
by Stanton A. Cobllentz

C-29 **THE GREEN MAN OF GRAYPEC**
by Festus Pragnell

C-30 **THE SHAVER MYSTERY, Book Four**
by Richard S. Shaver

ARMCHAIR MASTERS OF SCIENCE FICTION SERIES, $16.95 each

MS-7 **MASTERS OF SCIENCE FICTION AND FANTASY, Vol. Seven**
Lester del Rey, "The Band Played On" and other tales

MS-8 **MASTERS OF SCIENCE FICTION, Vol. Eight**
Milton Lesser, "'A' is for Android" and other tales

STRANDED IN A LAND OF PERPETUAL DAYLIGHT

It was called the mechanical mole, and inside of it, David Innes and Abner Perry bore through the world's crust and traveled hundreds of miles down toward the very center of the Earth itself. Most unexpectedly, they broke into a strange inner world—the land of Pellucidar.

Pellucidar was the land of eternal daylight. Its sun hung high above, perpetually immobile. It was a remarkable world where time and direction seemed not to exist. It was a world filled with prehistoric monstrosities, the likes of which Innes and Perry had only read about in science books. It was a place ruled by the dreaded Mahars. The Mahars—to whom human beings were nothing more than slaves.

Come along and face the many dangers of this fantastic world, the likes of which could only have been created by the brilliant mind of Edgar Rice Burroughs.

ABOUT EDGAR RICE BURROUGHS:

Edgar Rice Burroughs was born in Chicago in 1875. He is universall y acclaim ed for hi s amazing novels of science fiction, fantasy, and adventure. He is best known for Tarzan's jungle adventures, the wil ds of Pellucidar, and of course…John Carter's escapades on Mars.

Prior to his fame as a writer, Burroughs attempted a number of di fferent careers, but he met with littl e success. Then at the age of 35 he turned to writing. He achieved instant success with the publication of his two best known novels, *A Princess of Mars* and *Tarzan of the Apes*.

During hi s career, he wrote nearly seventy novels spanning many different genres. He was also a mainst ay in the pulp magazines of the '30s and '40s, often appearing i n *Amazing Stories* and *Fantastic Adventures*. During World War Two, in spite of his advanced age, he also gained fame as a successful war correspondent.

Burroughs left a beloved legacy of brilliant stories, a product of his seemingly endless imagination. Edgar Rice Burroughs died i n Tarzana, California on March 19th, 1950.

AT THE
EARTH'S
CORE

By
EDGAR RICE BURROUGHS

ARMCHAIR FICTION
PO Box 4369, Medford, Oregon   97501-0168

*For more information about Armchair Books and products, visit our
website at…*

www.armchairfiction.com

Or email us at…

armchairfiction@yahoo.com

PROLOGUE

IN THE FIRST PLACE PLEASE BEAR IN MIND THAT I do not expect you to believe this story. Nor could you wonder had you witnessed a recent experience of mine when, in the armor of blissful and stupendous ignorance, I gaily narrated the gist of it to a Fellow of the Royal Geological Society on the occasion of my last trip to London.

You would surely have thought that I had been detected in no less a heinous crime than the purloining of the Crown Jewels from the Tower, or putting poison in the coffee of His Majesty the King.

The erudite gentleman in whom I confided congealed before I was half through!—it is all that saved him from exploding—and my dreams of an Honorary Fellowship, gold medals, and a niche in the Hall of Fame faded into the thin, cold air of his arctic atmosphere.

But I believe the story, and so would you, and so would the learned Fellow of the Royal Geological Society, had you and he heard it from the lips of the man who told it to me. Had you seen, as I did, the fire of truth in those gray eyes; had you felt the ring of sincerity in that quiet voice; had you realized the pathos of it all—you, too, would believe. You would not have needed the final ocular proof that I had—the weird rhamphorhynchus-like creature which he had brought back with him from the inner world.

I came upon him quite suddenly, and no less unexpectedly, upon the rim of the great Sahara Desert. He was standing before a goat-skin tent amidst a clump of date palms within a tiny oasis. Close by was an Arab douar of some eight or ten tents.

I had come down from the north to hunt lion. My party consisted of a dozen children of the desert—I was the only "white" man. As we approached the little clump of verdure I saw the man come from his tent and with hand-shaded eyes peer intently at us. At sight of me he advanced rapidly to meet us.

"A white man!" he cried. "May the good Lord be praised! I have been watching you for hours, hoping against hope that THIS time there would be a white man. Tell me the date. What year is it?"

And when I had told him he staggered as though he had been struck full in the face, so that he was compelled to grasp my stirrup leather for support.

"It cannot be!" he cried after a moment. "It cannot be! Tell me that you are mistaken, or that you are but joking."

"I am telling you the truth, my friend," I replied. "Why should I deceive a stranger, or attempt to, in so simple a matter as the date?"

For some time he stood in silence, with bowed head.

"Ten years!" he murmured, at last. "Ten years, and I thought that at the most it could be scarce more than one!" That night he told me his story—the story that I give you here as nearly in his own words as I can recall them.

CHAPTER ONE
Toward the Eternal Fires

I WAS BORN IN CONNECTICUT ABOUT THIRTY YEARS ago. My name is David Innes. My father was a wealthy mine owner. When I was nineteen he died. All his property was to be mine when I had attained my majority—provided that I had devoted the two years intervening in close application to the great business I was to inherit.

I did my best to fulfil the last wishes of my parent—not because of the inheritance, but because I loved and honored my father. For six months I toiled in the mines and in the counting-rooms, for I wished to know every minute detail of the business.

Then Perry interested me in his invention. He was an old fellow who had devoted the better part of a long life to the perfection of a mechanical subterranean prospector. As relaxation he studied paleontology. I looked over his plans, listened to his arguments, inspected his working model—and then, convinced, I advanced the funds necessary to construct a full-sized, practical prospector.

I shall not go into the details of its construction—it lies out there in the desert now—about two miles from here. Tomorrow you may care to ride out and see it. Roughly, it is a steel cylinder a hundred feet long, and jointed so that it may turn and twist through solid rock if need be. At one end is a mighty revolving drill operated by an engine which Perry said generated more power to the cubic inch than any other engine did to the cubic foot. I remember that he used to claim that that invention alone would make us fabulously wealthy—we were going to make the whole thing public after the successful issue of our first secret trial—but Perry never returned from that trial trip, and I only after ten years.

I recall as it were but yesterday the night of that momentous occasion upon which we were to test the practicality of that wondrous invention. It was near midnight when we repaired to the lofty tower in which Perry had constructed his "iron mole" as he was wont to call the thing. The great nose rested upon the bare earth of the floor. We passed through the doors into the outer jacket, secured them, and then passing on into the cabin, which contained the controlling mechanism within the inner tube, switched on the electric lights.

Perry looked to his generator; to the great tanks that held the life-giving chemicals with which he was to manufacture fresh air to replace that which we consumed in breathing; to his instruments for recording temperatures, speed, distance, and for examining the materials through which we were to pass.

He tested the steering device, and overlooked the mighty cogs which transmitted its marvelous velocity to the giant drill at the nose of his strange craft.

Our seats, into which we strapped ourselves, were so arranged upon transverse bars that we would be upright whether the craft were ploughing her way downward into the bowels of the earth, or running horizontally along some great seam of coal, or rising vertically toward the surface again.

At length all was ready. Perry bowed his head in prayer. For a moment we were silent, and then the old man's hand grasped the starting lever. There was a frightful roaring beneath us—the giant frame trembled and vibrated—there was a rush of sound as the loose earth passed up through the hollow space between the inner and outer jackets to be deposited in our wake. We were off!

The noise was deafening. The sensation was frightful. For a full minute neither of us could do aught but cling with the proverbial desperation of the drowning man to the handrails of our swinging seats. Then Perry glanced at the thermometer.

"Gad!" he cried, "it cannot be possible—quick! What does the distance meter read?"

That and the speedometer were both on my side of the cabin, and as I turned to take a reading from the former I could see Perry muttering.

"Ten degrees rise—it cannot be possible!" and then I saw him tug frantically upon the steering wheel.

As I finally found the tiny needle in the dim light I translated Perry's evident excitement, and my heart sank within me. But when I spoke I hid the fear which haunted me. "It will be seven hundred feet, Perry," I said, "by the time you can turn her into the horizontal."

"You'd better lend me a hand then, my boy," he replied, "for I cannot budge her out of the vertical alone. God give that our combined strength may be equal to the task, for else we are lost."

I wormed my way to the old man's side with never a doubt but that the great wheel would yield on the instant to the power of my young and vigorous muscles. Nor was my belief mere vanity, for always had my physique been the envy and despair of my fellows. And for that very reason it had waxed even greater than nature had intended, since my natural pride in my great strength had led me to care for and develop my body and my muscles by every means within my power. What with boxing, football, and baseball, I had been in training since childhood.

And so it was with the utmost confidence that I laid hold of the huge iron rim; but though I threw every ounce of my strength into it, my best effort was as unavailing as Perry's had been—the thing would not budge—the grim, insensate, horrible thing that was holding us upon the straight road to death!

At length I gave up the useless struggle, and without a word returned to my seat. There was no need for words—at least none that I could imagine, unless Perry desired to pray. And I was quite sure that he would, for he never left an opportunity neglected where he might sandwich in a prayer. He prayed when he arose in the morning, he prayed before he ate, he prayed when he had finished eating, and before he went to bed at night he prayed again. In between he often found excuses to pray even when the provocation seemed far-fetched to my worldly eyes—now that he was about to die I felt positive that I should witness a perfect orgy of prayer—if one may allude with such a simile to so solemn an act.

But to my astonishment I discovered that with death staring him in the face Abner Perry was transformed into a new being. From his lips there flowed—not prayer—but a clear and limpid stream of undiluted profanity, and it was all directed at that quietly stubborn piece of unyielding mechanism.

"I should think, Perry," I chided, "that a man of your professed religiousness would rather be at his prayers than cursing in the presence of imminent death."

"Death!" he cried. "Death is it that appalls you? That is nothing by comparison with the loss the world must suffer. Why, David within this iron cylinder we have demonstrated possibilities that science has scarce dreamed. We have harnessed a new principle, and with it animated a piece of steel with the power of ten thousand men. That two lives will be snuffed out is nothing to the world calamity that entombs in the bowels of the earth the discoveries that I have made and proved in the successful construction of the thing that is now carrying us farther and farther toward the eternal central fires."

I am frank to admit that for myself I was much more concerned with our own immediate future than with any problematic loss which the world might be about to suffer. The world was at least ignorant of its bereavement, while to me it was a real and terrible actuality.

"What can we do?" I asked, hiding my perturbation beneath the mask of a low and level voice.

"We may stop here, and die of asphyxiation when our atmosphere tanks are empty," replied Perry, "or we may continue on with the slight hope that we may later sufficiently deflect the prospector from the vertical to carry us along the arc of a great circle which must eventually return us to the surface. If we succeed in so doing before we reach the higher internal temperature we may even yet survive. There would seem to me to be about one chance in several million that we shall succeed—otherwise we shall die more quickly but no more surely than as though we sat supinely waiting for the torture of a slow and horrible death."

I glanced at the thermometer. It registered 110 degrees. While we were talking the mighty iron mole had bored its way over a mile into the rock of the earth's crust.

"Let us continue on, then," I replied. "It should soon be over at this rate. You never intimated that the speed of this thing would be so high, Perry. Didn't you know it?"

"No," he answered. "I could not figure the speed exactly, for I had no instrument for measuring the mighty power of my generator. I reasoned, however, that we should make about five hundred yards an hour."

"And we are making seven miles an hour," I concluded for him, as I sat with my eyes upon the distance meter. "How thick is the Earth's crust, Perry?" I asked.

"There are almost as many conjectures as to that as there are geologists," was his answer. "One estimates it thirty miles, because the internal heat, increasing at the rate of about one degree to each sixty to seventy feet depth, would be sufficient to fuse the most refractory substances at that distance beneath the surface. Another finds that the phenomena of precession and nutation require that the earth, if not entirely solid, must at least have a shell not less than eight hundred to a thousand miles in thickness. So there you are. You may take your choice."

"And if it should prove solid?" I asked.

"It will be all the same to us in the end, David," replied Perry. "At the best our fuel will suffice to carry us but three or four days, while our atmosphere cannot last to exceed three. Neither, then, is sufficient to bear us in safety through eight thousand miles of rock to the antipodes."

"If the crust is of sufficient thickness we shall come to a final stop between six and seven hundred miles beneath the earth's surface; but during the last hundred and fifty miles of our journey we shall be corpses. Am I correct?" I asked.

"Quite correct, David. Are you frightened?"

"I do not know. It all has come so suddenly that I scarce believe that either of us realizes the real terrors of our position. I feel that I should be reduced to panic; but yet I am not. I imagine that the shock has been so great as to partially stun our sensibilities."

Again I turned to the thermometer. The mercury was rising with less rapidity. It was now but 140 degrees, although we had penetrated to a depth of nearly four miles. I told Perry, and he smiled.

"We have shattered one theory at least," was his only comment, and then he returned to his self-assumed occupation of fluently cursing the steering wheel. I once heard a pirate swear, but his best efforts would have seemed like those of a tyro alongside of Perry's masterful and scientific imprecations.

Once more I tried my hand at the wheel, but I might as well have essayed to swing the earth itself. At my suggestion Perry stopped the generator, and as we came to rest I again threw all my strength into a supreme effort to move the thing even a hair's breadth—but the results were as barren as when we had been traveling at top speed.

I shook my head sadly, and motioned to the starting lever. Perry pulled it toward him, and once again we were plunging downward toward eternity at the rate of seven miles an hour. I sat with my eyes glued to the thermometer and the distance meter. The mercury was rising very slowly now, though even at 145 degrees it was almost unbearable within the narrow confines of our metal prison.

About noon, or twelve hours after our start upon this unfortunate journey, we had bored to a depth of eighty-four miles, at which point the mercury registered 153 degrees F.

Perry was becoming more hopeful, although upon what meager food he sustained his optimism I could not conjecture. From cursing he had turned to singing—I felt that the strain had at last affected his mind. For several hours we had not spoken except as he asked me for the readings of the instruments from time to time, and I announced them. My thoughts were filled with vain regrets. I recalled numerous acts of my past life which I should have been glad to have had a few more years to live down. There was the affair in the Latin Commons at Andover when Calhoun and I had put gunpowder in the stove—and nearly killed one of the masters. And then—but what was the use, I was about to die and atone for all these things and several more. Already the heat was sufficient to give me a foretaste of the hereafter. A few more degrees and I felt that I should lose consciousness.

"What are the readings now, David?" Perry's voice broke in upon my somber reflections.

"Ninety miles and 153 degrees," I replied.

"Gad, but we've knocked that thirty-mile-crust theory into a cocked hat!" he cried gleefully.

"Precious lot of good it will do us," I growled back.

"But my boy," he continued, "doesn't that temperature reading mean anything to you? Why it hasn't gone up in six miles. Think of it, son!"

"Yes, I'm thinking of it," I answered; "but what difference will it make when our air supply is exhausted whether the temperature is 153 degrees or 153,000? We'll be just as dead, and no one will know the difference, anyhow." But I must admit that for some unaccountable reason the stationary temperature did renew my waning hope. What I hoped for I could not have explained, nor did I try. The very fact, as Perry took pains to explain, of the blasting of several very exact and learned scientific hypotheses made it apparent that we could not know what lay before us within the bowels of the earth, and so we might continue to hope for the best, at least until we were dead—when hope would no longer be essential to our happiness. It was very good, and logical reasoning, and so I embraced it.

At one hundred miles the temperature had DROPPED TO 152 1/2 DEGREES! When I announced it Perry reached over and hugged me.

From then on until noon of the second day, it continued to drop until it became as uncomfortably cold as it had been unbearably hot before. At the depth of two hundred and forty miles our nostrils were assailed by almost overpowering ammonia fumes, and the temperature had dropped to TEN BELOW ZERO! We suffered nearly two hours of this intense and bitter cold, until at about two hundred and forty-five miles from the surface of the earth we entered a stratum of solid ice, when the mercury quickly rose to 32 degrees. During the next three hours we passed through ten miles of ice, eventually emerging into another series of ammonia-impregnated strata, where the mercury again fell to ten degrees below zero.

Slowly it rose once more until we were convinced that at last we were nearing the molten interior of the earth. At four hundred miles the temperature had reached 153 degrees.

Feverishly I watched the thermometer. Slowly it rose. Perry had ceased singing and was at last praying.

Our hopes had received such a deathblow that the gradually increasing heat seemed to our distorted imaginations much greater than it really was. For another hour I saw that pitiless column of mercury rise and rise until at four hundred and ten miles it stood at 153 degrees. Now it was that we began to hang upon those readings in almost breathless anxiety.

One hundred and fifty-three degrees had been the maximum temperature above the ice stratum. Would it stop at this point again, or would it continue its merciless climb? We knew that there was no hope, and yet with the persistence of life itself we continued to hope against practical certainty.

Already the air tanks were at low ebb—there was barely enough of the precious gases to sustain us for another twelve hours. But would we be alive to know or care? It seemed incredible.

At four hundred and twenty miles I took another reading.

"Perry!" I shouted. "Perry, man! She's going down! She's going down! She's 152 degrees again."

"Gad!" he cried. "What can it mean? Can the earth be cold at the center?"

"I do not know, Perry," I answered; "but thank God, if I am to die it shall not be by fire—that is all that I have feared. I can face the thought of any death but that."

Down, down went the mercury until it stood as low as it had seven miles from the surface of the earth, and then of a sudden the realization broke upon us that death was very near. Perry was the first to discover it. I saw him fussing with the valves that regulate the air supply. And at the same time I experienced difficulty in breathing. My head felt dizzy—my limbs heavy.

I saw Perry crumple in his seat. He gave himself a shake and sat erect again. Then he turned toward me.

"Good-bye, David," he said. "I guess this is the end," and then he smiled and closed his eyes.

"Good-bye, Perry, and good luck to you," I answered, smiling back at him. But I fought off that awful lethargy. I was very young—I did not want to die.

For an hour I battled against the cruelly enveloping death that surrounded me upon all sides. At first I found that by climbing high into the framework above me I could find more of the precious life-giving elements, and for a while these sustained me. It must have been an hour after Perry had succumbed that I at last came to the realization that I could no longer carry on this unequal struggle against the inevitable.

With my last flickering ray of consciousness I turned mechanically toward the distance meter. It stood at exactly five hundred miles from the earth's surface—and then of a sudden the huge thing that bore us came to a stop. The rattle of hurtling rock through the hollow jacket ceased. The wild racing of the giant drill betokened that it was running loose in AIR— and then another truth flashed upon me. The point of the prospector was ABOVE us. Slowly it dawned on me that since passing through the ice strata it had been above. We had turned in the ice and sped upward toward the earth's crust. Thank God! We were safe!

I put my nose to the intake pipe through which samples were to have been taken during the passage of the prospector through the earth, and my fondest hopes were realized—a flood of fresh air was pouring into the iron cabin. The reaction left me in a state of collapse, and I lost consciousness.

CHAPTER TWO
A Strange World

I WAS UNCONSCIOUS LITTLE MORE THAN AN INSTANT, for as I lunged forward from the crossbeam to which I had been clinging, and fell with a crash to the floor of the cabin, the shock brought me to myself.

My first concern was with Perry. I was horrified at the thought that upon the very threshold of salvation he might be dead. Tearing open his shirt I placed my ear to his breast. I could have cried with relief—his heart was beating quite regularly.

At the water tank I wetted my handkerchief, slapping it smartly across his forehead and face several times. In a moment I was rewarded by the raising of his lids. For a time he lay wide-eyed and quite uncomprehending. Then his scattered wits slowly foregathered, and he sat up sniffing the air with an expression of wonderment upon his face.

"Why, David," he cried at last, "it's air, as sure as I live. Why—why what does it mean? Where in the world are we? What has happened?"

"It means that we're back at the surface all right, Perry," I cried; "but where, I don't know. I haven't opened her up yet. Been too busy reviving you. Lord, man, but you had a close squeak!"

"You say we're back at the surface, David? How can that be? How long have I been unconscious?"

"Not long. We turned in the ice stratum. Don't you recall the sudden whirling of our seats? After that the drill was above you instead of below. We didn't notice it at the time; but I recall it now."

"You mean to say that we turned back in the ice stratum, David? That is not possible. The prospector cannot turn unless its nose is deflected from the outside—by some external force or resistance—the steering wheel within would have moved in response. The steering wheel has not budged, David, since we started. You know that."

I did know it; but here we were with our drill racing in pure air, and copious volumes of it pouring into the cabin.

"We couldn't have turned in the ice stratum, Perry, I know as well as you," I replied; "but the fact remains that we did, for here we are this minute at the surface of the earth again, and I am going out to see just where."

"Better wait till morning, David—it must be midnight now."

I glanced at the chronometer.

"Half after twelve. We have been out seventy-two hours, so it must be midnight. Nevertheless I am going to have a look at the blessed sky that I had given up all hope of ever seeing again," and so saying I lifted the bars from the inner door, and swung it open. There was quite a quantity of loose material in the jacket, and this I had to remove with a shovel to get at the opposite door in the outer shell.

In a short time I had removed enough of the earth and rock to the floor of the cabin to expose the door beyond. Perry was directly behind me as I threw it open. The upper half was above the surface of the ground. With an expression of surprise I turned and looked at Perry—it was broad daylight without!

"Something seems to have gone wrong either with our calculations or the chronometer," I said. Perry shook his head—there was a strange expression in his eyes.

"Let's have a look beyond that door, David," he cried.

Together we stepped out to stand in silent contemplation of a landscape at once weird and beautiful. Before us a low and level shore stretched down to a silent sea. As far as the eye could reach the surface of the water was dotted with countless tiny isles—some of towering, barren, granitic rock—others resplendent in gorgeous trappings of tropical vegetation, myriad starred with the magnificent splendor of vivid blooms.

Behind us rose a dark and forbidding wood of giant arborescent ferns intermingled with the commoner types of a primeval tropical forest. Huge creepers depended in great loops from tree to tree, dense under-brush overgrew a tangled mass of fallen trunks and branches. Upon the outer verge we could see the same splendid coloring of countless blossoms that glorified the islands, but within the dense shadows all seemed dark and gloomy as the grave.

And upon all the noonday sun poured its torrid rays out of a cloudless sky.

"Where on earth can we be?" I asked, turning to Perry.

For some moments the old man did not reply. He stood with bowed head, buried in deep thought. But at last he spoke.

"David," he said, "I am not so sure that we are ON earth."

"What do you mean, Perry?" I cried. "Do you think that we are dead, and this is heaven?" He smiled, and turning, pointing to the nose of the prospector protruding from the ground at our backs.

"But for that, David, I might believe that we were indeed come to the country beyond the Styx. The prospector renders that theory untenable—it, certainly, could never have gone to heaven. However I am willing to concede that we actually may be in another world from that which we have always known. If we are not ON earth, there is every reason to believe that we may be IN it."

"We may have quartered through the earth's crust and come out upon some tropical island of the West Indies," I suggested. Again Perry shook his head.

"Let us wait and see, David," he replied, "and in the meantime suppose we do a bit of exploring up and down the coast—we may find a native who can enlighten us."

As we walked along the beach Perry gazed long and earnestly across the water. Evidently he was wrestling with a mighty problem.

"David," he said abruptly, "do you perceive anything unusual about the horizon?"

As I looked I began to appreciate the reason for the strangeness of the landscape that had haunted me from the first with an illusive suggestion of the bizarre and unnatural—THERE WAS NO HORIZON! As far as the eye could reach out the sea continued and upon its bosom floated tiny islands, those in the distance reduced to mere specks; but ever beyond them was the sea, until the impression became quite real that one was LOOKING UP at the most distant point that the eyes could fathom—the distance was lost in the distance. That was all—there was no clear-cut horizontal line marking the dip of the globe below the line of vision.

"A great light is commencing to break on me," continued Perry, taking out his watch. "I believe that I have partially solved the riddle. It is now two o'clock. When we emerged from the prospector the sun was directly above us. Where is it now?"

I glanced up to find the great orb still motionless in the center of the heaven. And such a sun! I had scarcely noticed it before. Fully thrice the size of the sun I had known throughout my life, and apparently so near that the sight of it carried the conviction that one might almost reach up and touch it.

"My God, Perry, where are we?" I exclaimed. "This thing is beginning to get on my nerves."

"I think that I may state quite positively, David," he commenced, "that we are—" but he got no further. From behind us in the vicinity of the prospector there came the most thunderous, awe-inspiring roar that ever had fallen upon my ears. With one accord we turned to discover the author of that fearsome noise.

Had I still retained the suspicion that we were on earth the sight that met my eyes would quite entirely have banished it. Emerging from the forest was a colossal beast which closely resembled a bear. It was fully as large as the largest elephant and with great forepaws armed with huge claws. Its nose, or snout, depended nearly a foot below its lower jaw, much after the manner of a rudimentary trunk. The giant body was covered by a coat of thick, shaggy hair.

Roaring horribly it came toward us at a ponderous, shuffling trot. I turned to Perry to suggest that it might be wise to seek other surroundings—the idea had evidently occurred to Perry previously, for he was already a hundred paces away, and with each second his prodigious bounds increased the distance. I had never guessed what latent speed possibilities the old gentleman possessed.

I saw that he was headed toward a little point of the forest which ran out toward the sea not far from where we had been standing, and as the mighty creature, the sight of which had galvanized him into such remarkable action, was forging steadily toward me, I set off after Perry, though at a somewhat more decorous pace. It was evident that the massive beast pursuing us was not built for speed, so all that I considered necessary was to gain the trees sufficiently ahead of it to enable me to climb to the safety of some great branch before it came up.

Notwithstanding our danger I could not help but laugh at Perry's frantic capers as he essayed to gain the safety of the lower branches of the trees he now had reached. The stems were bare for a distance of some fifteen feet—at least on those trees which Perry attempted to ascend, for the suggestion of safety carried by the larger of the forest giants had evidently attracted him to them. A dozen times he scrambled up the trunks like a huge cat only to fall back to the ground once more, and with each failure he cast a horrified glance over his shoulder at the oncoming brute, simultaneously emitting terror-stricken shrieks that awoke the echoes of the grim forest.

At length he spied a dangling creeper about the bigness of one's wrist, and when I reached the trees he was racing madly up it, hand over hand. He had almost reached the lowest branch of the tree from which the creeper depended when the thing parted beneath his weight and he fell sprawling at my feet.

The misfortune now was no longer amusing, for the beast was already too close to us for comfort. Seizing Perry by the shoulder I dragged him to his feet, and rushing to a smaller tree—one that he could easily encircle with his arms and legs—I boosted him as far up as I could, and then left him to his fate, for a glance over my shoulder revealed the awful beast almost upon me.

It was the great size of the thing alone that saved me. Its enormous bulk rendered it too slow upon its feet to cope with the agility of my young muscles, and so I was enabled to dodge out of its way and run completely behind it before its slow wits could direct it in pursuit.

The few seconds of grace that this gave me found me safely lodged in the branches of a tree a few paces from that in which Perry had at last found a haven.

Did I say safely lodged? At the time I thought we were quite safe, and so did Perry. He was praying—raising his voice in thanksgiving at our deliverance—and had just completed a sort of paeon of gratitude that the thing couldn't climb a tree when without warning it reared up beneath him on its enormous tail and hind feet, and reached those fearfully armed paws quite to the branch upon which he crouched.

The accompanying roar was all but drowned in Perry's scream of fright, and he came near tumbling headlong into the gaping jaws beneath him, so precipitate was his impetuous haste to vacate the dangerous limb. It was with a deep sigh of relief that I saw him gain a higher branch in safety.

And then the brute did that which froze us both anew with horror. Grasping the tree's stem with his powerful paws he dragged down with all the great weight of his huge bulk and all the irresistible force of those mighty muscles. Slowly, but surely, the stem began to bend toward him. Inch by inch he worked his paws upward as the tree leaned more and more from the perpendicular. Perry clung chattering in a panic of terror. Higher and higher into the bending and swaying tree he clambered. More and more rapidly was the tree top inclining toward the ground.

I saw now why the great brute was armed with such enormous paws. The use that he was putting them to was precisely that for which nature had intended them. The sloth-like creature was herbivorous, and to feed that mighty carcass entire trees must be stripped of their foliage. The reason for its attacking us might easily be accounted for on the supposition of an ugly disposition such as that which the fierce and stupid rhinoceros of Africa possesses. But these were later reflections. At the moment I was too frantic with apprehension on Perry's behalf to consider aught other than a means to save him from the death that loomed so close.

Realizing that I could outdistance the clumsy brute in the open, I dropped from my leafy sanctuary intent only on distracting the thing's attention from Perry long enough to enable the old man to gain the safety of a larger tree. There were many close by which not even the terrific strength of that titanic monster could bend.

As I touched the ground I snatched a broken limb from the tangled mass that matted the jungle-like floor of the forest and, leaping unnoticed behind the shaggy back, dealt the brute a terrific blow. My plan worked like magic. From the previous slowness of the beast I had been led to look for no such marvelous agility as he now displayed. Releasing his hold upon the tree he dropped on all fours and at the same time swung his great, wicked tail with a force that would have broken every bone in my body had it struck me; but, fortunately, I had turned to flee at the very instant that I felt my blow land upon the towering back.

As it started in pursuit of me I made the mistake of running along the edge of the forest rather than making for the open beach. In a moment I was knee-deep in rotting vegetation, and the awful thing behind me was gaining rapidly as I floundered and fell in my efforts to extricate myself.

A fallen log gave me an instant's advantage, for climbing upon it I leaped to another a few paces farther on, and in this way was able to keep clear of the mush that carpeted the surrounding ground. But the zigzag course that this necessitated was placing such a heavy handicap upon me that my pursuer was steadily gaining upon me.

Suddenly from behind I heard a tumult of howls, and sharp, piercing barks—much the sound that a pack of wolves raises when in full cry. Involuntarily I glanced backward to discover the origin of this new and menacing note with the result that I missed my footing and went sprawling once more upon my face in the deep muck.

My mammoth enemy was so close by this time that I knew I must feel the weight of one of his terrible paws before I could rise, but to my surprise the blow did not fall upon me. The howling and snapping and barking of the new element which had been infused into the melee now seemed centered quite close behind me, and as I raised myself upon my hands and glanced around I saw what it was that had distracted the DYRYTH, as I afterward learned the thing is called, from my trail.

It was surrounded by a pack of some hundred wolf-like creatures—wild dogs they seemed—that rushed growling and snapping in upon it from all sides, so that they sank their white fangs into the slow brute and were away again before it could reach them with its huge paws or sweeping tail.

But these were not all that my startled eyes perceived. Chattering and gibbering through the lower branches of the trees came a company of manlike creatures evidently urging on the dog pack. They were to all appearances strikingly similar in aspect to the Negro of Africa. Their skins were very black, and their features much like those of the more pronounced Negroid type except that the head receded more rapidly above the eyes, leaving little or no forehead. Their arms were rather longer and their legs shorter in proportion to the torso than in man, and later I noticed that their great toes protruded at right angles from their feet—because of their arboreal habits, I presume. Behind them trailed long, slender tails which they used in climbing quite as much as they did either their hands or feet.

I had stumbled to my feet the moment that I discovered that the wolf-dogs were holding the dyryth at bay. At sight of me several of the savage creatures left off worrying the great brute to come slinking with bared fangs toward me, and as I turned to run toward the trees again to seek safety among the lower branches, I saw a number of the man-apes leaping and chattering in the foliage of the nearest tree.

Between them and the beasts behind me there was little choice, but at least there was a doubt as to the reception these grotesque parodies on humanity would accord me, while there was none as to the fate which awaited me beneath the grinning fangs of my fierce pursuers.

And so I raced on toward the trees intending to pass beneath that which held the man-things and take refuge in another farther on; but the wolf-dogs were very close behind me—so close that I had despaired of escaping them, when one of the creatures in the tree above swung down headforemost, his tail looped about a great limb, and grasping me beneath my armpits swung me in safety up among his fellows.

There they fell to examining me with the utmost excitement and curiosity. They picked at my clothing, my hair, and my flesh. They turned me about to see if I had a tail, and when they discovered that I was not so equipped they fell into roars of laughter. Their teeth were very large and white and even, except for the upper canines which were a trifle longer than the others—protruding just a bit when the mouth was closed.

When they had examined me for a few moments one of them discovered that my clothing was not a part of me, with the result that garment by garment they tore it from me amidst peals of the wildest laughter. Apelike, they essayed to don the apparel themselves, but their ingenuity was not sufficient to the task and so they gave it up.

In the meantime I had been straining my eyes to catch a glimpse of Perry, but nowhere about could I see him, although the clump of trees in which he had first taken refuge was in full view. I was much exercised by fear that something had befallen him, and though I called his name aloud several times there was no response.

Tired at last of playing with my clothing the creatures threw it to the ground, and catching me, one on either side, by an arm, started off at a most terrifying pace through the tree tops. Never have I experienced such a journey before or since—even now I oftentimes awake from a deep sleep haunted by the horrid remembrance of that awful experience.

From tree to tree the agile creatures sprang like flying squirrels, while the cold sweat stood upon my brow as I glimpsed the depths beneath, into which a single misstep on the part of either of my bearers would hurl me. As they bore me along, my mind was occupied with a thousand bewildering thoughts. What had become of Perry? Would I ever see him again? What were the intentions of these half-human things into whose hands I had fallen? Were they inhabitants of the same world into which I had been born? No! It could not be. But yet where else? I had not left that earth—of that I was sure. Still neither could I reconcile the things which I had seen to a belief that I was still in the world of my birth. With a sigh I gave it up.

CHAPTER THREE
A Change of Masters

WE MUST HAVE TRAVELED SEVERAL MILES THROUGH the dark and dismal wood when we came suddenly upon a dense village built high among the branches of the trees. As we approached it my escort broke into wild shouting which was immediately answered from within, and a moment later a swarm of creatures of the same strange race as those who had captured me poured out to meet us. Again I was the center of a wildly chattering horde. I was pulled this way and that. Pinched, pounded, and thumped until I was black and blue, yet I do not think that their treatment was dictated by either cruelty or malice—I was a curiosity, a freak, a new plaything, and their childish minds required the added evidence of all their senses to back up the testimony of their eyes.

Presently they dragged me within the village, which consisted of several hundred rude shelters of boughs and leaves supported upon the branches of the trees.

Between the huts, which sometimes formed crooked streets, were dead branches and the trunks of small trees which connected the huts upon one tree to those within adjoining trees; the whole network of huts and pathways forming an almost solid flooring a good fifty feet above the ground.

I wondered why these agile creatures required connecting bridges between the trees, but later when I saw the motley aggregation of half-savage beasts which they kept within their village I realized the necessity for the pathways. There were a number of the same vicious wolf-dogs which we had left worrying the dyryth, and many goatlike animals whose distended udders explained the reasons for their presence.

My guard halted before one of the huts into which I was pushed; then two of the creatures squatted down before the entrance—to prevent my escape, doubtless. Though where I should have escaped to I certainly had not the remotest conception. I had no more than entered the dark shadows of the interior than there fell upon my ears the tones of a familiar voice, in prayer.

"Perry!" I cried. "Dear old Perry! Thank the Lord you are safe."

"David! Can it be possible that you escaped?" And the old man stumbled toward me and threw his arms about me.

He had seen me fall before the dyryth, and then he had been seized by a number of the ape-creatures and borne through the tree tops to their village. His captors had been as inquisitive as to his strange clothing as had mine, with the same result. As we looked at each other we could not help but laugh.

"With a tail, David," remarked Perry, "you would make a very handsome ape."

"Maybe we can borrow a couple," I rejoined. "They seem to be quite the thing this season. I wonder what the creatures intend doing with us, Perry. They don't seem really savage. What do you suppose they can be? You were about to tell me where we are when that great hairy frigate bore down upon us— have you really any idea at all?"

"Yes, David," he replied, "I know precisely where we are. We have made a magnificent discovery, my boy! We have proved that the earth is hollow. We have passed entirely through its crust to the inner world."

"Perry, you are mad!"

"Not at all, David. For two hundred and fifty miles our prospector bore us through the crust beneath our outer world. At that point it reached the center of gravity of the five-hundred-mile-thick crust. Up to that point we had been descending—direction is, of course, merely relative. Then at the moment that our seats revolved—the thing that made you believe that we had turned about and were speeding upward—we passed the center of gravity and, though we did not alter the direction of our progress, yet we were in reality moving upward—toward the surface of the inner world. Does not the strange fauna and flora which we have seen convince you that you are not in the world of your birth? And the horizon—could it present the strange aspects which we both noted unless we were indeed standing upon the inside surface of a sphere?"

"But the sun, Perry!" I urged. "How in the world can the sun shine through five hundred miles of solid crust?"

"It is not the sun of the outer world that we see here. It is another sun—an entirely different sun—that casts its eternal noonday effulgence upon the face of the inner world. Look at it now, David—if you can see it from the doorway of this hut—and you will see that it is still in the exact center of the heavens. We have been here for many hours—yet it is still noon.

"And withal it is very simple, David. The earth was once a nebulous mass. It cooled, and as it cooled it shrank. At length a thin crust of solid matter formed upon its outer surface—a sort of shell; but within it was partially molten matter and highly expanded gases. As it continued to cool, what happened? Centrifugal force hurled the particles of the nebulous center toward the crust as rapidly as they approached a solid state. You have seen the same principle practically applied in the modern cream separator. Presently there was only a small super-heated core of gaseous matter remaining within a huge vacant interior left by the contraction of the cooling gases. The equal attraction of the solid crust from all directions maintained this luminous core in the exact center of the hollow globe. What remains of it is the sun you saw today—a relatively tiny thing at the exact center of the earth. Equally to every part of this inner world it diffuses its perpetual noonday light and torrid heat.

"This inner world must have cooled sufficiently to support animal life long ages after life appeared upon the outer crust, but that the same agencies were at work here is evident from the similar forms of both animal and vegetable creation which we have already seen. Take the great beast which attacked us, for example. Unquestionably a counterpart of the Megatherium of the post-Pliocene period of the outer crust, whose fossilized skeleton has been found in South America."

"But the grotesque inhabitants of this forest?" I urged. "Surely they have no counterpart in the earth's history."

"Who can tell?" he rejoined. "They may constitute the link between ape and man, all traces of which have been swallowed by the countless convulsions which have racked the outer crust, or they may be merely the result of evolution along slightly different lines—either is quite possible."

Further speculation was interrupted by the appearance of several of our captors before the entrance of the hut. Two of them entered and dragged us forth. The perilous pathways and the surrounding trees were filled with the black ape-men, their females, and their young. There was not an ornament, a weapon, or a garment among the lot.

"Quite low in the scale of creation," commented Perry.

"Quite high enough to play the deuce with us, though," I replied. "Now what do you suppose they intend doing with us?"

We were not long in learning. As on the occasion of our trip to the village we were seized by a couple of the powerful creatures and whirled away through the tree tops, while about us and in our wake raced a chattering, jabbering, grinning horde of sleek, black ape-things.

Twice my bearers missed their footing, and my heart ceased beating as we plunged toward instant death among the tangled deadwood beneath. But on both occasions those lithe, powerful tails reached out and found sustaining branches, nor did either of the creatures loosen their grasp upon me. In fact, it seemed that the incidents were of no greater moment to them than would be the stubbing of one's toe at a street crossing in the outer world—they but laughed uproariously and sped on with me.

For some time they continued through the forest—how long I could not guess for I was learning, what was later borne very forcefully to my mind, that time ceases to be a factor the moment means for measuring it cease to exist. Our watches were gone, and we were living beneath a stationary sun. Already I was puzzled to compute the period of time which had elapsed since we broke through the crust of the inner world. It might be hours, or it might be days—who in the world could tell where it was always noon! By the sun, no time had elapsed—but my judgment told me that we must have been several hours in this strange world.

Presently the forest terminated, and we came out upon a level plain. A short distance before us rose a few low, rocky hills. Toward these our captors urged us, and after a short time led us through a narrow pass into a tiny, circular valley. Here they got down to work, and we were soon convinced that if we were not to die to make a Roman holiday, we were to die for some other purpose. The attitude of our captors altered immediately as they entered the natural arena within the rocky hills. Their laughter ceased. Grim ferocity marked their bestial faces—bared fangs menaced us.

We were placed in the center of the amphitheater—the thousand creatures forming a great ring about us. Then a wolf-dog was brought—HYAENODON Perry called it—and turned loose with us inside the circle. The thing's body was as large as that of a full-grown mastiff, its legs were short and powerful, and its jaws broad and strong. Dark, shaggy hair covered its back and sides, while its breast and belly were quite white. As it slunk toward us it presented a most formidable aspect with its upcurled lips baring its mighty fangs.

Perry was on his knees, praying. I stooped and picked up a small stone. At my movement the beast veered off a bit and commenced circling us. Evidently it had been a target for stones before. The ape-things were dancing up and down urging the brute on with savage cries, until at last, seeing that I did not throw, he charged us.

At Andover, and later at Yale, I had pitched on winning ball teams. My speed and control must both have been above the ordinary, for I made such a record during my senior year at college that overtures were made to me in behalf of one of the great major-league teams; but in the tightest pitch that ever had confronted me in the past I had never been in such need for control as now.

As I wound up for the delivery, I held my nerves and muscles under absolute command, though the grinning jaws were hurtling toward me at terrific speed. And then I let go, with every ounce of my weight and muscle and science in back of that throw. The stone caught the hyaenodon full upon the end of the nose, and sent him bowling over upon his back.

At the same instant a chorus of shrieks and howls arose from the circle of spectators, so that for a moment I thought that the upsetting of their champion was the cause; but in this I soon saw that I was mistaken. As I looked, the ape-things broke in all directions toward the surrounding hills, and then I distinguished the real cause of their perturbation. Behind them, streaming through the pass which leads into the valley, came a swarm of hairy men—gorilla-like creatures armed with spears and hatchets, and bearing long, oval shields. Like demons they set upon the ape-things, and before them the hyaenodon, which had now regained its senses and its feet, fled howling with fright. Past us swept the pursued and the pursuers, nor did the hairy ones accord us more than a passing glance until the arena had been emptied of its former occupants. Then they returned to us, and one who seemed to have authority among them directed that we be brought with them.

When we had passed out of the amphitheater onto the great plain we saw a caravan of men and women—human beings like ourselves—and for the first time hope and relief filled my heart, until I could have cried out in the exuberance of my happiness. It is true that they were a half-naked, wild-appearing aggregation; but they at least were fashioned along the same lines as ourselves—there was nothing grotesque or horrible about them as about the other creatures in this strange, weird world.

But as we came closer, our hearts sank once more, for we discovered that the poor wretches were chained neck to neck in a long line, and that the gorilla-men were their guards. With little ceremony Perry and I were chained at the end of the line, and without further ado the interrupted march was resumed.

Up to this time the excitement had kept us both up; but now the tiresome monotony of the long march across the sun-baked plain brought on all the agonies consequent to a long-denied sleep. On and on we stumbled beneath that hateful noonday sun. If we fell we were prodded with a sharp point. Our companions in chains did not stumble. They strode along proudly erect. Occasionally they would exchange words with one another in a monosyllabic language. They were a noble-appearing race with well-formed heads and perfect physiques. The men were heavily bearded, tall and muscular; the women, smaller and more gracefully molded, with great masses of raven hair caught into loose knots upon their heads. The features of both sexes were well proportioned—there was not a face among them that would have been called even plain if judged by earthly standards. They wore no ornaments; but this I later learned was due to the fact that their captors had stripped them of everything of value. As garmenture the women possessed a single robe of some light-colored, spotted hide, rather similar in appearance to a leopard's skin. This they wore either supported entirely about the waist by a leathern thong, so that it hung partially below the knee on one side, or possibly looped gracefully across one shoulder. Their feet were shod with skin sandals. The men wore loin cloths of the hide of some shaggy beast, long ends of which depended before and behind nearly to the ground. In some instances these ends were finished with the strong talons of the beast from which the hides had been taken.

Our guards, whom I already have described as gorilla-like men, were rather lighter in build than a gorilla, but even so they were indeed mighty creatures. Their arms and legs were proportioned more in conformity with human standards, but their entire bodies were covered with shaggy, brown hair, and their faces were quite as brutal as those of the few stuffed specimens of the gorilla which I had seen in the museums at home.

Their only redeeming feature lay in the development of the head above and back of the ears. In this respect they were not one whit less human than we. They were clothed in a sort of tunic of light cloth which reached to the knees. Beneath this they wore only a loin cloth of the same material, while their feet were shod with thick hide of some mammoth creature of this inner world.

Their arms and necks were encircled by many ornaments of metal—silver predominating—and on their tunics were sewn the heads of tiny reptiles in odd and rather artistic designs. They talked among themselves as they marched along on either side of us, but in a language which I perceived differed from that employed by our fellow prisoners. When they addressed the latter they used what appeared to be a third language, and which I later learned is a mongrel tongue rather analogous to the Pidgin-English of the Chinese coolie.

How far we marched I have no conception, nor has Perry. Both of us were asleep much of the time for hours before a halt was called—then we dropped in our tracks. I say "for hours," but how may one measure time where time does not exist! When our march commenced the sun stood at zenith. When we halted our shadows still pointed toward nadir. Whether an instant or an eternity of earthly time elapsed who may say. That march may have occupied nine years and eleven months of the ten years that I spent in the inner world, or it may have been accomplished in the fraction of a second—I cannot tell. But this I do know that since you have told me that ten years have elapsed since I departed from this earth I have lost all respect for time—I am commencing to doubt that such a thing exists other than in the weak, finite mind of man.

CHAPTER FOUR
Dian the Beautiful

WHEN OUR GUARDS AROUSED US FROM SLEEP WE were much refreshed. They gave us food. Strips of dried meat it was, but it put new life and strength into us, so that now we too marched with high-held heads, and took noble strides. At least I did, for I was young and proud; but poor Perry hated walking. On earth I had often seen him call a cab to travel a square—he was paying for it now, and his old legs wobbled so that I put my arm about him and half carried him through the balance of those frightful marches.

The country began to change at last, and we wound up out of the level plain through mighty mountains of virgin granite. The tropical verdure of the lowlands was replaced by hardier vegetation, but even here the effects of constant heat and light were apparent in the immensity of the trees and the profusion of foliage and blooms. Crystal streams roared through their rocky channels, fed by the perpetual snows which we could see far above us. Above the snowcapped heights hung masses of heavy clouds. It was these, Perry explained, which evidently served the double purpose of replenishing the melting snows and protecting them from the direct rays of the sun.

By this time we had picked up a smattering of the bastard language in which our guards addressed us, as well as making good headway in the rather charming tongue of our co-captives. Directly ahead of me in the chain gang was a young woman. Three feet of chain linked us together in a forced companionship which I, at least, soon rejoiced in. For I found her a willing teacher, and from her I learned the language of her tribe, and much of the life and customs of the inner world—at least that part of it with which she was familiar.

She told me that she was called Dian the Beautiful, and that she belonged to the tribe of Amoz, which dwells in the cliffs above the Darel Az, or shallow sea.

"How came you here?" I asked her.

"I was running away from Jubal the Ugly One," she answered, as though that was explanation quite sufficient.

"Who is Jubal the Ugly One?" I asked. "And why did you run away from him?"

She looked at me in surprise.

"Why DOES a woman run away from a man?" she answered my question with another.

"They do not, where I come from," I replied. "Sometimes they run after them."

But she could not understand. Nor could I get her to grasp the fact that I was of another world. She was quite as positive that creation was originated solely to produce her own kind and the world she lived in as are many of the outer world.

"But Jubal," I insisted. "Tell me about him, and why you ran away to be chained by the neck and scourged across the face of a world."

"Jubal the Ugly One placed his trophy before my father's house. It was the head of a mighty tandor. It remained there and no greater trophy was placed beside it. So I knew that Jubal the Ugly One would come and take me as his mate. None other so powerful wished me, or they would have slain a mightier beast and thus have won me from Jubal. My father is not a mighty hunter. Once he was, but a sadok tossed him, and never again had he the full use of his right arm. My brother, Dacor the Strong One, had gone to the land of Sari to steal a mate for himself. Thus there was none, father, brother, or lover, to save me from Jubal the Ugly One, and I ran away and hid among the hills that skirt the land of Amoz. And there these Sagoths found me and made me captive."

"What will they do with you?" I asked. "Where are they taking us?"

Again she looked her incredulity.

"I can almost believe that you are of another world," she said, "for otherwise such ignorance were inexplicable. Do you really mean that you do not know that the Sagoths are the creatures of the Mahars—the mighty Mahars who think they own Pellucidar and all that walks or grows upon its surface, or creeps or burrows beneath, or swims within its lakes and oceans, or flies through its air? Next you will be telling me that you never before heard of the Mahars!"

I was loath to do it, and further incur her scorn; but there was no alternative if I were to absorb knowledge, so I made a clean breast of my pitiful ignorance as to the mighty Mahars. She was shocked. But she did her very best to enlighten me, though much that she said was as Greek would have been to her. She described the Mahars largely by comparisons. In this way they were like unto thipdars, in that to the hairless lidi.

About all I gleaned of them was that they were quite hideous, had wings, and webbed feet; lived in cities built beneath the ground; could swim under water for great distances, and were very, very wise. The Sagoths were their weapons of offense and defense, and the races like herself were their hands and feet—they were the slaves and servants who did all the manual labor. The Mahars were the heads—the brains—of the inner world. I longed to see this wondrous race of supermen.

Perry learned the language with me. When we halted, as we occasionally did, though sometimes the halts seemed ages apart, he would join in the conversation, as would Ghak the Hairy One, he who was chained just ahead of Dian the Beautiful. Ahead of Ghak was Hooja the Sly One. He too entered the conversation occasionally. Most of his remarks were directed toward Dian the Beautiful. It didn't take half an eye to see that he had developed a bad case; but the girl appeared totally oblivious to his thinly veiled advances. Did I say thinly veiled? There is a race of men in New Zealand, or Australia, I have forgotten which, who indicate their preference for the lady of their affections by banging her over the head with a bludgeon. By comparison with this method Hooja's lovemaking might be called thinly veiled. At first it caused me to blush violently although I have seen several Old Years out at Rectors, and in other less fashionable places off Broadway, and in Vienna, and Hamburg.

But the girl! She was magnificent. It was easy to see that she considered herself as entirely above and apart from her present surroundings and company. She talked with me, and with Perry, and with the taciturn Ghak because we were respectful; but she couldn't even see Hooja the Sly One, much less hear him, and that made him furious. He tried to get one of the Sagoths to move the girl up ahead of him in the slave gang, but the fellow only poked him with his spear and told him that he had selected the girl for his own property—that he would buy her from the Mahars as soon as they reached Phutra. Phutra, it seemed, was the city of our destination.

After passing over the first chain of mountains we skirted a salt sea, upon whose bosom swam countless horrid things. Seal-like creatures there were with long necks stretching ten and more feet above their enormous bodies and whose snake heads were split with gaping mouths bristling with countless fangs. There were huge tortoises too, paddling about among these other reptiles, which Perry said were Plesiosaurs of the Lias. I didn't question his veracity—they might have been most anything.

Dian told me they were tandorazes, or tandors of the sea, and that the other, and more fearsome reptiles, which occasionally rose from the deep to do battle with them, were azdyryths, or sea-dyryths—Perry called them Ichthyosaurs. They resembled a whale with the head of an alligator.

I had forgotten what little geology I had studied at school—about all that remained was an impression of horror that the illustrations of restored prehistoric monsters had made upon me, and a well-defined belief that any man with a pig's shank and a vivid imagination could "restore" most any sort of paleolithic monster he saw fit, and take rank as a first class paleontologist. But when I saw these sleek, shiny carcasses shimmering in the sunlight as they emerged from the ocean, shaking their giant heads; when I saw the waters roll from their sinuous bodies in miniature waterfalls as they glided hither and thither, now upon the surface, now half submerged; as I saw them meet, open-mouthed, hissing and snorting, in their titanic and interminable warring I realized how futile is man's poor, weak imagination by comparison with Nature's incredible genius.

And Perry! He was absolutely flabbergasted. He said so himself.

"David," he remarked, after we had marched for a long time beside that awful sea. "David, I used to teach geology, and I thought that I believed what I taught; but now I see that I did not believe it—that it is impossible for man to believe such things as these unless he sees them with his own eyes. We take things for granted, perhaps, because we are told them over and over again, and have no way of disproving them—like religions, for example; but we don't believe them, we only think we do. If you ever get back to the outer world you will find that the geologists and paleontologists will be the first to set you down a liar, for they know that no such creatures as they restore ever existed. It is all right to IMAGINE them as existing in an equally imaginary epoch—but now? poof!"

At the next halt Hooja the Sly One managed to find enough slack chain to permit him to worm himself back quite close to Dian. We were all standing, and as he edged near the girl she turned her back upon him in such a truly earthly feminine manner that I could scarce repress a smile; but it was a short-lived smile for on the instant the Sly One's hand fell upon the girl's bare arm, jerking her roughly toward him.

I was not then familiar with the customs or social ethics which prevailed within Pellucidar; but even so I did not need the appealing look which the girl shot to me from her magnificent eyes to influence my subsequent act. What the Sly One's intention was I paused not to inquire; but instead, before he could lay hold of her with his other hand, I placed a right to the point of his jaw that felled him in his tracks.

A roar of approval went up from those of the other prisoners and the Sagoths who had witnessed the brief drama; not, as I later learned, because I had championed the girl, but for the neat and, to them, astounding method by which I had bested Hooja.

And the girl? At first she looked at me with wide, wondering eyes, and then she dropped her head, her face half averted, and a delicate flush suffused her cheek. For a moment she stood thus in silence, and then her head went high, and she turned her back upon me as she had upon Hooja. Some of the prisoners laughed, and I saw the face of Ghak the Hairy One go very black as he looked at me searchingly. And what I could see of Dian's cheek went suddenly from red to white.

Immediately after we resumed the march, and though I realized that in some way I had offended Dian the Beautiful I could not prevail upon her to talk with me that I might learn wherein I had erred—in fact I might quite as well have been addressing a sphinx for all the attention I got. At last my own foolish pride stepped in and prevented my making any further attempts, and thus a companionship that without my realizing it had come to mean a great deal to me was cut off. Thereafter I confined my conversation to Perry. Hooja did not renew his advances toward the girl, nor did he again venture near me.

Again the weary and apparently interminable marching became a perfect nightmare of horrors to me. The more firmly fixed became the realization that the girl's friendship had meant so much to me, the more I came to miss it; and the more impregnable the barrier of silly pride. But I was very young and would not ask Ghak for the explanation which I was sure he could give, and that might have made everything all right again.

On the march, or during halts, Dian refused consistently to notice me—when her eyes wandered in my direction she looked either over my head or directly through me. At last I became desperate, and determined to swallow my self-esteem, and again beg her to tell me how I had offended, and how I might make reparation. I made up my mind that I should do this at the next halt. We were approaching another range of mountains at the time, and when we reached them, instead of winding across them through some high-flung pass we entered a mighty natural tunnel—a series of labyrinthine grottoes, dark as Erebus.

The guards had no torches or light of any description. In fact we had seen no artificial light or sign of fire since we had entered Pellucidar. In a land of perpetual noon there is no need of light above ground, yet I marveled that they had no means of lighting their way through these dark, subterranean passages. So we crept along at a snail's pace, with much stumbling and falling—the guards keeping up a singsong chant ahead of us, interspersed with certain high notes which I found always indicated rough places and turns.

Halts were now more frequent, but I did not wish to speak to Dian until I could see from the expression of her face how she was receiving my apologies. At last a faint glow ahead forewarned us of the end of the tunnel, for which I for one was devoutly thankful. Then at a sudden turn we emerged into the full light of the noonday sun.

But with it came a sudden realization of what meant to me a real catastrophe—Dian was gone, and with her a half-dozen other prisoners. The guards saw it too, and the ferocity of their rage was terrible to behold. Their awesome, bestial faces were contorted in the most diabolical expressions, as they accused each other of responsibility for the loss. Finally they fell upon us, beating us with their spear shafts, and hatchets. They had already killed two near the head of the line, and were like to have finished the balance of us when their leader finally put a stop to the brutal slaughter. Never in all my life had I witnessed a more horrible exhibition of bestial rage—I thanked God that Dian had not been one of those left to endure it.

Of the twelve prisoners who had been chained ahead of me each alternate one had been freed commencing with Dian. Hooja was gone. Ghak remained. What could it mean? How had it been accomplished? The commander of the guards was investigating. Soon he discovered that the rude locks which had held the neckbands in place had been deftly picked.

"Hooja the Sly One," murmured Ghak, who was now next to me in line. "He has taken the girl that you would not have," he continued, glancing at me.

"That I would not have!" I cried. "What do you mean?"

He looked at me closely for a moment.

"I have doubted your story that you are from another world," he said at last, "but yet upon no other grounds could your ignorance of the ways of Pellucidar be explained. Do you really mean that you do not know that you offended the Beautiful One, and how?"

"I do not know, Ghak," I replied.

"Then shall I tell you. When a man of Pellucidar intervenes between another man and the woman the other man would have, the woman belongs to the victor. Dian the Beautiful belongs to you. You should have claimed her or released her. Had you taken her hand, it would have indicated your desire to make her your mate, and had you raised her hand above her head and then dropped it, it would have meant that you did not wish her for a mate and that you released her from all obligation to you. By doing neither you have put upon her the greatest affront that a man may put upon a woman. Now she is your slave. No man will take her as mate, or may take her honorably, until he shall have overcome you in combat, and men do not choose slave women as their mates—at least not the men of Pellucidar."

"I did not know, Ghak," I cried. "I did not know. Not for all Pellucidar would I have harmed Dian the Beautiful by word, or look, or act of mine. I do not want her as my slave. I do not want her as my—" but here I stopped. The vision of that sweet and innocent face floated before me amidst the soft mists of imagination, and where I had on the second believed that I clung only to the memory of a gentle friendship I had lost, yet now it seemed that it would have been disloyalty to her to have said that I did not want Dian the Beautiful as my mate. I had not thought of her except as a welcome friend in a strange, cruel world. Even now I did not think that I loved her.

I believe Ghak must have read the truth more in my expression than in my words, for presently he laid his hand upon my shoulder.

"Man of another world," he said, "I believe you. Lips may lie, but when the heart speaks through the eyes it tells only the truth. Your heart has spoken to me. I know now that you meant no affront to Dian the Beautiful. She is not of my tribe; but her mother is my sister. She does not know it—her mother was stolen by Dian's father who came with many others of the tribe of Amoz to battle with us for our women—the most beautiful women of Pellucidar. Then was her father king of Amoz, and her mother was daughter of the king of Sari—to whose power I, his son, have succeeded. Dian is the daughter of kings, though her father is no longer king since the sadok tossed him and Jubal the Ugly One wrested his kingship from him. Because of her lineage the wrong you did her was greatly magnified in the eyes of all who saw it. She will never forgive you."

I asked Ghak if there was not some way in which I could release the girl from the bondage and ignominy I had unwittingly placed upon her.

"If ever you find her, yes," he answered. "Merely to raise her hand above her head and drop it in the presence of others is sufficient to release her; but how may you ever find her, you who are doomed to a life of slavery yourself in the buried city of Phutra?"

"Is there no escape?" I asked.

"Hooja the Sly One escaped and took the others with him," replied Ghak. "But there are no more dark places on the way to Phutra, and once there it is not so easy—the Mahars are very wise. Even if one escaped from Phutra there are the thipdars—they would find you, and then—" the Hairy One shuddered. "No, you will never escape the Mahars."

It was a cheerful prospect. I asked Perry what he thought about it; but he only shrugged his shoulders and continued a longwinded prayer he had been at for some time. He was wont to say that the only redeeming feature of our captivity was the ample time it gave him for the improvisation of prayers—it was becoming an obsession with him. The Sagoths had begun to take notice of his habit of declaiming throughout entire marches. One of them asked him what he was saying—to whom he was talking. The question gave me an idea, so I answered quickly before Perry could say anything.

"Do not interrupt him," I said. "He is a very holy man in the world from which we come. He is speaking to spirits which you cannot see—do not interrupt him or they will spring out of the air upon you and rend you limb from limb—like that," and I jumped toward the great brute with a loud "Boo!" that sent him stumbling backward.

I took a long chance, I realized, but if we could make any capital out of Perry's harmless mania I wanted to make it while the making was prime. It worked splendidly. The Sagoths treated us both with marked respect during the balance of the journey, and then passed the word along to their masters, the Mahars.

Two marches after this episode we came to the city of Phutra. The entrance to it was marked by two lofty towers of granite, which guarded a flight of steps leading to the buried city. Sagoths were on guard here as well as at a hundred or more other towers scattered about over a large plain.

CHAPTER FIVE
Slaves

AS WE DESCENDED THE BROAD STAIRCASE WHICH led to the main avenue of Phutra I caught my first sight of the dominant race of the inner world. Involuntarily I shrank back as one of the creatures approached to inspect us. A more hideous thing it would be impossible to imagine. The all-powerful Mahars of Pellucidar are great reptiles, some six or eight feet in length, with long narrow heads and great round eyes. Their beak-like mouths are lined with sharp, white fangs, and the backs of their huge, lizard bodies are serrated into bony ridges from their necks to the end of their long tails. Their feet are equipped with three webbed toes, while from the fore feet membranous wings, which are attached to their bodies just in front of the hind legs, protrude at an angle of 45 degrees toward the rear, ending in sharp points several feet above their bodies.

I glanced at Perry as the thing passed me to inspect him. The old man was gazing at the horrid creature with wide astonished eyes. When it passed on, he turned to me.

"A rhamphorhynchus of the Middle Olitic, David," he said, "but, gad, how enormous! The largest remains we ever have discovered have never indicated a size greater than that attained by an ordinary crow."

As we continued on through the main avenue of Phutra we saw many thousand of the creatures coming and going upon their daily duties. They paid but little attention to us. Phutra is laid out underground with a regularity that indicates remarkable engineering skill. It is hewn from solid limestone strata. The streets are broad and of a uniform height of twenty feet. At intervals tubes pierce the roof of this underground city, and by means of lenses and reflectors transmit the sunlight, softened and diffused, to dispel what would otherwise be Cimmerian darkness. In like manner air is introduced.

Perry and I were taken, with Ghak, to a large public building, where one of the Sagoths who had formed our guard explained to a Maharan official the circumstances surrounding our capture. The method of communication between these two was remarkable in that no spoken words were exchanged. They employed a species of sign language. As I was to learn later, the Mahars have no ears, not any spoken language. Among themselves they communicate by means of what Perry says must be a sixth sense which is cognizant of a fourth dimension.

I never did quite grasp him, though he endeavored to explain it to me upon numerous occasions. I suggested telepathy, but he said no, that it was not telepathy since they could only communicate when in each others' presence, nor could they talk with the Sagoths or the other inhabitants of Pellucidar by the same method they used to converse with one another.

"What they do," said Perry, "is to project their thoughts into the fourth dimension, when they become appreciable to the sixth sense of their listener. Do I make myself quite clear?"

"You do not, Perry," I replied. He shook his head in despair, and returned to his work. They had set us to carrying a great accumulation of Maharan literature from one apartment to another, and there arranging it upon shelves. I suggested to Perry that we were in the public library of Phutra, but later, as he commenced to discover the key to their written language, he assured me that we were handling the ancient archives of the race.

During this period my thoughts were continually upon Dian the Beautiful. I was, of course, glad that she had escaped the Mahars, and the fate that had been suggested by the Sagoth who had threatened to purchase her upon our arrival at Phutra. I often wondered if the little party of fugitives had been overtaken by the guards who had returned to search for them. Sometimes I was not so sure but that I should have been more contented to know that Dian was here in Phutra, than to think of her at the mercy of Hooja the Sly One. Ghak, Perry, and I often talked together of possible escape, but the Sarian was so steeped in his lifelong belief that no one could escape from the Mahars except by a miracle, that he was not much aid to us—his attitude was of one who waits for the miracle to come to him.

At my suggestion Perry and I fashioned some swords of scraps of iron which we discovered among some rubbish in the cells where we slept, for we were permitted almost unrestrained freedom of action within the limits of the building to which we had been assigned. So great were the number of slaves who waited upon the inhabitants of Phutra that none of us was apt to be overburdened with work, nor were our masters unkind to us.

We hid our new weapons beneath the skins which formed our beds, and then Perry conceived the idea of making bows and arrows—weapons apparently unknown within Pellucidar. Next came shields; but these I found it easier to steal from the walls of the outer guardroom of the building.

We had completed these arrangements for our protection after leaving Phutra when the Sagoths who had been sent to recapture the escaped prisoners returned with four of them, of whom Hooja was one. Dian and two others had eluded them. It so happened that Hooja was confined in the same building with us. He told Ghak that he had not seen Dian or the others after releasing them within the dark grotto. What had become of them he had not the faintest conception—they might be wandering yet, lost within the labyrinthine tunnel, if not dead from starvation.

I was now still further apprehensive as to the fate of Dian, and at this time, I imagine, came the first realization that my affection for the girl might be prompted by more than friendship. During my waking hours she was constantly the subject of my thoughts, and when I slept her dear face haunted my dreams. More than ever was I determined to escape the Mahars.

"Perry," I confided to the old man, "if I have to search every inch of this diminutive world I am going to find Dian the Beautiful and right the wrong I unintentionally did her." That was the excuse I made for Perry's benefit.

"Diminutive world!" he scoffed. "You don't know what you are talking about, my boy," and then he showed me a map of Pellucidar which he had recently discovered among the manuscript he was arranging.

"Look," he cried, pointing to it, "this is evidently water, and all this land. Do you notice the general configuration of the two areas? Where the oceans are upon the outer crust, is land here.

These relatively small areas of ocean follow the general lines of the continents of the outer world.

"We know that the crust of the globe is 500 miles in thickness; then the inside diameter of Pellucidar must be 7,000 miles, and the superficial area 165,480,000 square miles. Three-fourths of this is land. Think of it! A land area of 124,110,000 square miles! Our own world contains but 53,000,000 square miles of land, the balance of its surface being covered by water. Just as we often compare nations by their relative land areas, so if we compare these two worlds in the same way we have the strange anomaly of a larger world within a smaller one!

"Where within vast Pellucidar would you search for your Dian? Without stars, or moon, or changing sun how could you find her even though you knew where she might be found?"

The proposition was a corker. It quite took my breath away; but I found that it left me all the more determined to attempt it.

"If Ghak will accompany us we may be able to do it," I suggested.

Perry and I sought him out and put the question straight to him.

"Ghak," I said, "we are determined to escape from this bondage. Will you accompany us?"

"They will set the thipdars upon us," he said, "and then we shall be killed; but..." He hesitated. "...I would take the chance if I thought that I might possibly escape and return to my own people."

"Could you find your way back to your own land?" asked Perry. "And could you aid David in his search for Dian?"

"Yes."

"But how," persisted Perry, "could you travel to strange country without heavenly bodies or a compass to guide you?"

Ghak didn't know what Perry meant by heavenly bodies or a compass, but he assured us that you might blindfold any man of Pellucidar and carry him to the farthermost corner of the world, yet he would be able to come directly to his own home again by the shortest route. He seemed surprised to think that we found anything wonderful in it. Perry said it must be some sort of homing instinct such as is possessed by certain breeds of earthly pigeons. I didn't know, of course, but it gave me an idea.

"Then Dian could have found her way directly to her own people?" I asked.

"Surely," replied Ghak, "unless some mighty beast of prey killed her."

I was for making the attempted escape at once, but both Perry and Ghak counseled waiting for some propitious accident which would insure us some small degree of success. I didn't see what accident could befall a whole community in a land of perpetual daylight where the inhabitants had no fixed habits of sleep. Why, I am sure that some of the Mahars never sleep, while others may, at long intervals, crawl into the dark recesses beneath their dwellings and curl up in protracted slumber. Perry says that if a Mahar stays awake for three years he will make up all his lost sleep in a long year's snooze. That may be all true, but I never saw but three of them asleep, and it was the sight of these three that gave me a suggestion for our means of escape.

I had been searching about far below the levels that we slaves were supposed to frequent—possibly fifty feet beneath the main floor of the building—among a network of corridors and apartments, when I came suddenly upon three Mahars curled up upon a bed of skins. At first I thought they were dead, but later their regular breathing convinced me of my error. Like a flash the thought came to me of the marvelous opportunity these sleeping reptiles offered as a means of eluding the watchfulness of our captors and the Sagoth guards.

Hastening back to Perry where he pored over a musty pile of, to me, meaningless hieroglyphics, I explained my plan to him. To my surprise he was horrified.

"It would be murder, David," he cried.

"Murder to kill a reptilian monster?" I asked in astonishment.

"Here they are not monsters, David," he replied. "Here they are the dominant race—we are the 'monsters'—the lower orders. In Pellucidar evolution has progressed along different lines than upon the outer earth. These terrible convulsions of nature time and time again wiped out the existing species—but for this fact some monster of the Saurozoic epoch might rule today upon our own world. We see here what might well have occurred in our own history had conditions been what they have been here.

"Life within Pellucidar is far younger than upon the outer crust. Here man has but reached a stage analogous to the Stone Age of our own world's history, but for countless millions of years these reptiles have been progressing. Possibly it is the sixth sense which I am sure they possess that has given them an advantage over the other and more frightfully armed of their fellows; but this we may never know. They look upon us as we look upon the beasts of our fields, and I learn from their written records that other races of Mahars feed upon men—they keep them in great droves, as we keep cattle. They breed them most carefully, and when they are quite fat, they kill and eat them."

I shuddered.

"What is there horrible about it, David?" the old man asked. "They understand us no better than we understand the lower animals of our own world. Why, I have come across here very learned discussions of the question as to whether gilaks, that is men, have any means of communication. One writer claims that we do not even reason—that our every act is mechanical, or instinctive. The dominant race of Pellucidar, David, have not yet learned that men converse among themselves, or reason. Because we do not converse as they do it is beyond them to imagine that we converse at all. It is thus that we reason in relation to the brutes of our own world. They know that the Sagoths have a spoken language, but they cannot comprehend it, or how it manifests itself, since they have no auditory apparatus. They believe that the motions of the lips alone convey the meaning. That the Sagoths can communicate with us is incomprehensible to them.

"Yes, David," he concluded, "it would entail murder to carry out your plan."

"Very well then, Perry." I replied. "I shall become a murderer."

He got me to go over the plan again most carefully, and for some reason which was not at the time clear to me insisted upon a very careful description of the apartments and corridors I had just explored.

"I wonder, David," he said at length, "as you are determined to carry out your wild scheme, if we could not accomplish something of very real and lasting benefit for the human race of Pellucidar at the same time. Listen, I have learned much of a most surprising nature from these archives of the Mahars. That you may appreciate my plan I shall briefly outline the history of the race.

"Once the males were all-powerful, but ages ago the females, little by little, assumed the mastery. For other ages no noticeable change took place in the race of Mahars. It continued to progress under the intelligent and beneficent rule of the ladies. Science took vast strides. This was especially true of the sciences which we know as biology and eugenics. Finally a certain female scientist announced the fact that she had discovered a method whereby eggs might be fertilized by chemical means after they were laid—all true reptiles, you know, are hatched from eggs.

"What happened? Immediately the necessity for males ceased to exist—the race was no longer dependent upon them. More ages elapsed until at the present time we find a race consisting exclusively of females. But here is the point. The secret of this chemical formula is kept by a single race of Mahars. It is in the city of Phutra, and unless I am greatly in error I judge from your description of the vaults through which you passed today that it lies hidden in the cellar of this building.

"For two reasons they hide it away and guard it jealously. First, because upon it depends the very life of the race of Mahars, and second, owing to the fact that when it was public property as at first so many were experimenting with it that the danger of over-population became very grave.

"David, if we can escape, and at the same time take with us this great secret what will we not have accomplished for the human race within Pellucidar!" The very thought of it fairly overpowered me. Why, we two would be the means of placing the men of the inner world in their rightful place among created things. Only the Sagoths would then stand between them and absolute supremacy, and I was not quite sure but that the Sagoths owed all their power to the greater intelligence of the Mahars—I could not believe that these gorilla-like beasts were the mental superiors of the human race of Pellucidar.

"Why, Perry," I exclaimed, "you and I may reclaim a whole world! Together we can lead the races of men out of the darkness of ignorance into the light of advancement and civilization. At one step we may carry them from the Age of Stone to the twentieth century. It's marvelous—absolutely marvelous just to think about it."

"David," said the old man, "I believe that God sent us here for just that purpose—it shall be my life work to teach them His word—to lead them into the light of His mercy while we are training their hearts and hands in the ways of culture and civilization."

"You are right, Perry," I said, "and while you are teaching them to pray I'll be teaching them to fight, and between us we'll make a race of men that will be an honor to us both."

Ghak had entered the apartment some time before we concluded our conversation, and now he wanted to know what we were so excited about. Perry thought we had best not tell him too much, and so I only explained that I had a plan for escape. When I had outlined it to him, he seemed about as horror-struck as Perry had been; but for a different reason. The Hairy One only considered the horrible fate that would be ours were we discovered; but at last I prevailed upon him to accept my plan as the only feasible one, and when I had assured him that I would take all the responsibility for it were we captured, he accorded a reluctant assent.

CHAPTER SIX
The Beginning of Horror

WITHIN PELLUCIDAR ONE TIME IS AS GOOD AS ANOTHER. There were no nights to mask our attempted escape. All must be done in broad daylight—all but the work I had to do in the apartment beneath the building. So we determined to put our plan to an immediate test lest the Mahars who made it possible should awake before I reached them; but we were doomed to disappointment, for no sooner had we reached the main floor of the building on our way to the pits beneath, than we encountered hurrying bands of slaves being hastened under strong Sagoth guard out of the edifice to the avenue beyond.

Other Sagoths were darting hither and thither in search of other slaves, and the moment that we appeared we were pounced upon and hustled into the line of marching humans.

What the purpose or nature of the general exodus we did not know, but presently through the line of captives ran the rumor that two escaped slaves had been recaptured—a man and a woman—and that we were marching to witness their punishment, for the man had killed a Sagoth of the detachment that had pursued and overtaken them.

At the intelligence my heart sprang to my throat, for I was sure that the two were of those who escaped in the dark grotto with Hooja the Sly One, and that Dian must be the woman. Ghak thought so too, as did Perry.

"Is there naught that we may do to save her?" I asked Ghak.

"Naught," he replied.

Along the crowded avenue we marched, the guards showing unusual cruelty toward us, as though we, too, had been implicated in the murder of their fellow. The occasion was to serve as an object-lesson to all other slaves of the danger and futility of attempted escape, and the fatal consequences of taking the life of a superior being, and so I imagine that Sagoths felt amply justified in making the entire proceeding as uncomfortable and painful to us as possible.

They jabbed us with their spears and struck at us with the hatchets at the least provocation, and at no provocation at all. It was a most uncomfortable half-hour that we spent before we were finally herded through a low entrance into a huge building the center of which was given up to a good-sized arena. Benches surrounded this open space upon three sides, and along the fourth were heaped huge bowlders which rose in receding tiers toward the roof.

At first I couldn't make out the purpose of this mighty pile of rock, unless it were intended as a rough and picturesque background for the scenes which were enacted in the arena before it, but presently, after the wooden benches had been pretty well filled by slaves and Sagoths, I discovered the purpose of the bowlders, for then the Mahars began to file into the enclosure.

They marched directly across the arena toward the rocks upon the opposite side, where, spreading their bat-like wings, they rose above the high wall of the pit, settling down upon the bowlders above. These were the reserved seats, the boxes of the elect.

Reptiles that they are, the rough surface of a great stone is to them as plush as upholstery to us. Here they lolled, blinking their hideous eyes, and doubtless conversing with one another in their sixth-sense-fourth-dimension language.

For the first time I beheld their queen. She differed from the others in no feature that was appreciable to my earthly eyes, in fact all Mahars look alike to me; but when she crossed the arena after the balance of her female subjects had found their bowlders, she was preceded by a score of huge Sagoths, the largest I ever had seen, and on either side of her waddled a huge thipdar, while behind came another score of Sagoth guardsmen.

At the barrier the Sagoths clambered up the steep side with truly apelike agility, while behind them the haughty queen rose upon her wings with her two frightful dragons close beside her, and settled down upon the largest bowlder of them all in the exact center of that side of the amphitheater which is reserved for the dominant race. Here she squatted, a most repulsive and uninteresting queen; though doubtless quite as well assured of her beauty and divine right to rule as the proudest monarch of the outer world.

And then the music started—music without sound! The Mahars cannot hear, so the drums and fifes and horns of earthly bands are unknown among them. The "band" consists of a score or more Mahars. It filed out in the center of the arena where the creatures upon the rocks might see it, and there it performed for fifteen or twenty minutes.

Their technic consisted in waving their tails and moving their heads in a regular succession of measured movements resulting in a cadence which evidently pleased the eye of the Mahar as the cadence of our own instrumental music pleases our ears. Sometimes the band took measured steps in unison to one side or the other, or backward and again forward—it all seemed very silly and meaningless to me, but at the end of the first piece the Mahars upon the rocks showed the first indications of enthusiasm that I had seen displayed by the dominant race of Pellucidar. They beat their great wings up and down, and smote their rocky perches with their mighty tails until the ground shook. Then the band started another piece, and all was again as silent as the grave. That was one great beauty about Mahar music—if you didn't happen to like a piece that was being played all you had to do was shut your eyes.

When the band had exhausted its repertory it took wing and settled upon the rocks above and behind the queen. Then the business of the day was on. A man and woman were pushed into the arena by a couple of Sagoth guardsmen. I leaned forward in my seat to scrutinize the female—hoping against hope that she might prove to be another than Dian the Beautiful. Her back was toward me for a while, and the sight of the great mass of raven hair piled high upon her head filled me with alarm.

Presently a door in one side of the arena wall was opened to admit a huge, shaggy, bull-like creature.

"A Bos," whispered Perry, excitedly. "His kind roamed the outer crust with the cave bear and the mammoth ages and ages ago. We have been carried back a million years, David, to the childhood of a planet—is it not wondrous?"

But I saw only the raven hair of a half-naked girl, and my heart stood still in dumb misery at the sight of her, nor had I any eyes for the wonders of natural history. But for Perry and Ghak I should have leaped to the floor of the arena and shared whatever fate lay in store for this priceless treasure of the Stone Age.

With the advent of the Bos—they call the thing a thag within Pellucidar—two spears were tossed into the arena at the feet of the prisoners. It seemed to me that a bean shooter would have been as effective against the mighty monster as these pitiful weapons.

As the animal approached the two, bellowing and pawing the ground with the strength of many earthly bulls, another door directly beneath us was opened, and from it issued the most terrific roar that ever had fallen upon my outraged ears. I could not at first see the beast from which emanated this fearsome challenge, but the sound had the effect of bringing the two victims around with a sudden start, and then I saw the girl's face—she was not Dian! I could have wept for relief.

And now, as the two stood frozen in terror, I saw the author of that fearsome sound creeping stealthily into view. It was a huge tiger—such as hunted the great Bos through the jungles primeval when the world was young. In contour and markings it was not unlike the noblest of the Bengals of our own world, but as its dimensions were exaggerated to colossal proportions so too were its colorings exaggerated. Its vivid yellows fairly screamed aloud; its whites were as eider down; its blacks glossy as the finest anthracite coal, and its coat long and shaggy as a mountain goat. That it is a beautiful animal there is no gainsaying, but if its size and colors are magnified here within

Pellucidar, so is the ferocity of its disposition. It is not the occasional member of its species that is a man hunter—all are man hunters; but they do not confine their foraging to man alone, for there is no flesh or fish within Pellucidar that they will not eat with relish in the constant efforts which they make to furnish their huge carcasses with sufficient sustenance to maintain their mighty thews.

Upon one side of the doomed pair the thag bellowed and advanced, and upon the other tarag, the frightful, crept toward them with gaping mouth and dripping fangs.

The man seized the spears, handing one of them to the woman. At the sound of the roaring of the tiger the bull's bellowing became a veritable frenzy of rageful noise. Never in my life had I heard such an infernal din as the two brutes made, and to think it was all lost upon the hideous reptiles for whom the show was staged!

The thag was charging now from one side, and the tarag from the other. The two puny things standing between them seemed already lost, but at the very moment that the beasts were upon them the man grasped his companion by the arm and together they leaped to one side, while the frenzied creatures came together like locomotives in collision.

There ensued a battle royal which for sustained and frightful ferocity transcends the power of imagination or description. Time and again the colossal bull tossed the enormous tiger high into the air, but each time that the huge cat touched the ground he returned to the encounter with apparently undiminished strength, and seemingly increased ire.

For a while the man and woman busied themselves only with keeping out of the way of the two creatures, but finally I saw them separate and each creep stealthily toward one of the combatants. The tiger was now upon the bull's broad back, clinging to the huge neck with powerful fangs while its long, strong talons ripped the heavy hide into shreds and ribbons.

For a moment the bull stood bellowing and quivering with pain and rage, its cloven hoofs widespread, its tail lashing viciously from side to side, and then, in a mad orgy of bucking it went careening about the arena in frenzied attempt to unseat its rending rider. It was with difficulty that the girl avoided the first mad rush of the wounded animal.

All its efforts to rid itself of the tiger seemed futile, until in desperation it threw itself upon the ground, rolling over and over. A little of this so disconcerted the tiger, knocking its breath from it I imagine, that it lost its hold and then, quick as a cat, the great thag was up again and had buried those mighty horns deep in the tarag's abdomen, pinning him to the floor of the arena.

The great cat clawed at the shaggy head until eyes and ears were gone, and naught but a few strips of ragged, bloody flesh remained upon the skull. Yet through all the agony of that fearful punishment the thag still stood motionless pinning down his adversary, and then the man leaped in, seeing that the blind bull would be the least formidable enemy, and ran his spear through the tarag's heart.

As the animal's fierce clawing ceased, the bull raised his gory, sightless head, and with a horrid roar ran headlong across the arena. With great leaps and bounds he came, straight toward the arena wall directly beneath where we sat, and then accident carried him, in one of his mighty springs, completely over the barrier into the midst of the slaves and Sagoths just in front of us. Swinging his bloody horns from side to side the beast cut a wide swath before him straight upward toward our seats. Before him slaves and gorilla-men fought in mad stampede to escape the menace of the creature's death agonies, for such only could that frightful charge have been.

Forgetful of us, our guards joined in the general rush for the exits, many of which pierced the wall of the amphitheater behind us. Perry, Ghak, and I became separated in the chaos which reigned for a few moments after the beast cleared the wall of the arena, each intent upon saving his own hide.

I ran to the right, passing several exits choked with the fear mad mob that were battling to escape. One would have thought that an entire herd of thags was loose behind them, rather than a single blinded, dying beast; but such is the effect of panic upon a crowd.

CHAPTER SEVEN
Freedom

ONCE OUT OF THE DIRECT PATH OF THE ANIMAL, fear of it left me, but another emotion as quickly gripped me—hope of escape that the demoralized condition of the guards made possible for the instant.

I thought of Perry, and but for the hope that I might better encompass his release if myself free I should have put the thought of freedom from me at once. As it was I hastened on toward the right searching for an exit toward which no Sagoths were fleeing, and at last I found it—a low, narrow aperture leading into a dark corridor.

Without thought of the possible consequence, I darted into the shadows of the tunnel, feeling my way along through the gloom for some distance. The noises of the amphitheater had grown fainter and fainter until now all was as silent as the tomb about me. Faint light filtered from above through occasional ventilating and lighting tubes, but it was scarce sufficient to enable my human eyes to cope with the darkness, and so I was forced to move with extreme care, feeling my way along step by step with a hand upon the wall beside me.

Presently the light increased and a moment later, to my delight, I came upon a flight of steps leading upward, at the top of which the brilliant light of the noonday sun shone through an opening in the ground.

Cautiously I crept up the stairway to the tunnel's end, and peering out saw the broad plain of Phutra before me. The numerous lofty, granite towers which mark the several entrances to the subterranean city were all in front of me—behind, the plain stretched level and unbroken to the nearby foothills. I had come to the surface, then, beyond the city, and my chances for escape seemed much enhanced.

My first impulse was to await darkness before attempting to cross the plain, so deeply implanted are habits of thought; but of a sudden I recollected the perpetual noonday brilliance which envelops Pellucidar, and with a smile I stepped forth into the daylight.

Rank grass, waist high, grows upon the plain of Phutra—the gorgeous flowering grass of the inner world, each particular blade of which is tipped with a tiny, five-pointed blossom— brilliant little stars of varying colors that twinkle in the green foliage to add still another charm to the weird, yet lovely, landscape.

But then the only aspect which attracted me was the distant hills in which I hoped to find sanctuary, and so I hastened on, trampling the myriad beauties beneath my hurrying feet. Perry says that the force of gravity is less upon the surface of the inner world than upon that of the outer. He explained it all to me once, but I was never particularly brilliant in such matters and so most of it has escaped me. As I recall it the difference is due in some part to the counter-attraction of that portion of the earth's crust directly opposite the spot upon the face of Pellucidar at which one's calculations are being made. Be that as it may, it always seemed to me that I moved with greater speed and agility within Pellucidar than upon the outer surface—there was a certain airy lightness of step that was most pleasing, and a feeling of bodily detachment which I can only compare with that occasionally experienced in dreams.

And as I crossed Phutra's flower-bespangled plain that time I seemed almost to fly, though how much of the sensation was due to Perry's suggestion and how much to actuality I am sure I do not know. The more I thought of Perry the less pleasure I took in my new-found freedom. There could be no liberty for me within Pellucidar unless the old man shared it with me, and only the hope that I might find some way to encompass his release kept me from turning back to Phutra.

Just how I was to help Perry I could scarce imagine, but I hoped that some fortuitous circumstance might solve the problem for me. It was quite evident however that little less than a miracle could aid me, for what could I accomplish in this strange world, naked and unarmed? It was even doubtful that I could retrace my steps to Phutra should I once pass beyond view of the plain, and even were that possible, what aid could I bring to Perry no matter how far I wandered?

The case looked more and more hopeless the longer I viewed it, yet with a stubborn persistency I forged ahead toward the foothills. Behind me no sign of pursuit developed, before me I saw no living thing. It was as though I moved through a dead and forgotten world.

I have no idea, of course, how long it took me to reach the limit of the plain, but at last I entered the foothills, following a pretty little canyon upward toward the mountains. Beside me frolicked a laughing brooklet, hurrying upon its noisy way down to the silent sea. In its quieter pools I discovered many small fish, of four-or five-pound weight I should imagine. In appearance, except as to size and color, they were not unlike the whale of our own seas. As I watched them playing about I discovered, not only that they suckled their young, but that at intervals they rose to the surface to breathe as well as to feed upon certain grasses and a strange, scarlet lichen which grew upon the rocks just above the water line.

It was this last habit that gave me the opportunity I craved to capture one of these herbivorous cetaceans—that is what Perry calls them—and make as good a meal as one can on raw, warm-blooded fish; but I had become rather used, by this time, to the eating of food in its natural state, though I still balked on the eyes and entrails, much to the amusement of Ghak, to whom I always passed these delicacies.

Crouching beside the brook, I waited until one of the diminutive purple whales rose to nibble at the long grasses which overhung the water, and then, like the beast of prey that man really is, I sprang upon my victim, appeasing my hunger while he yet wriggled to escape.

Then I drank from the clear pool, and after washing my hands and face continued my flight. Above the source of the brook I encountered a rugged climb to the summit of a long ridge. Beyond was a steep declivity to the shore of a placid, inland sea, upon the quiet surface of which lay several beautiful islands.

The view was charming in the extreme, and as no man or beast was to be seen that might threaten my new-found liberty, I slid over the edge of the bluff, and half sliding, half falling, dropped into the delightful valley, the very aspect of which seemed to offer a haven of peace and security.

The gently sloping beach along which I walked was thickly strewn with strangely shaped, colored shells; some empty, others still housing as varied a multitude of mollusks as ever might have drawn out their sluggish lives along the silent shores of the antediluvian seas of the outer crust. As I walked I could not but compare myself with the first man of that other world, so complete the solitude which surrounded me, so primal and untouched the virgin wonders and beauties of adolescent nature. I felt myself a second Adam wending my lonely way through the childhood of a world, searching for my Eve, and at the thought there rose before my mind's eye the exquisite outlines of a perfect face surmounted by a loose pile of wondrous, raven hair.

As I walked, my eyes were bent upon the beach so that it was not until I had come quite upon it that I discovered that which shattered all my beautiful dream of solitude and safety and peace and primal overlordship. The thing was a hollowed log drawn upon the sands, and in the bottom of it lay a crude paddle.

The rude shock of awakening to what doubtless might prove some new form of danger was still upon me when I heard a rattling of loose stones from the direction of the bluff, and turning my eyes in that direction I beheld the author of the disturbance, a great copper-colored man, running rapidly toward me.

There was that in the haste with which he came which seemed quite sufficiently menacing, so that I did not need the added evidence of brandishing spear and scowling face to warn me that I was in no safe position, but whither to flee was indeed a momentous question.

The speed of the fellow seemed to preclude the possibility of escaping him upon the open beach. There was but a single alternative—the rude skiff—and with a celerity which equaled his, I pushed the thing into the sea and as it floated gave a final shove and clambered in over the end.

A cry of rage rose from the owner of the primitive craft, and an instant later his heavy, stone-tipped spear grazed my shoulder and buried itself in the bow of the boat beyond. Then I grasped the paddle, and with feverish haste urged the awkward, wobbly thing out upon the surface of the sea.

A glance over my shoulder showed me that the copper-colored one had plunged in after me and was swimming rapidly in pursuit. His mighty strokes bade fair to close up the distance between us in short order, for at best I could make but slow progress with my unfamiliar craft, which nosed stubbornly in every direction but that which I desired to follow, so that fully half my energy was expended in turning its blunt prow back into the course.

I had covered some hundred yards from shore when it became evident that my pursuer must grasp the stern of the skiff within the next half-dozen strokes. In a frenzy of despair, I bent to the grandfather of all paddles in a hopeless effort to escape, and still the copper giant behind me gained and gained.

His hand was reaching upward for the stern when I saw a sleek, sinuous body shoot from the depths below. The man saw it too, and the look of terror that overspread his face assured me that I need have no further concern as to him, for the fear of certain death was in his look.

And then about him coiled the great, slimy folds of a hideous monster of that prehistoric deep—a mighty serpent of the sea, with fanged jaws, and darting forked tongue, with bulging eyes, and bony protuberances upon head and snout that formed short, stout horns.

As I looked at that hopeless struggle my eyes met those of the doomed man, and I could have sworn that in his I saw an expression of hopeless appeal. But whether I did or not there swept through me a sudden compassion for the fellow. He was indeed a brother-man, and that he might have killed me with pleasure had he caught me was forgotten in the extremity of his danger.

Unconsciously I had ceased paddling as the serpent rose to engage my pursuer, so now the skiff still drifted close beside the two. The monster seemed to be but playing with his victim before he closed his awful jaws upon him and dragged him down to his dark den beneath the surface to devour him. The huge, snakelike body coiled and uncoiled about its prey. The hideous, gaping jaws snapped in the victim's face. The forked tongue, lightning-like, ran in and out upon the copper skin.

Nobly the giant battled for his life, beating with his stone hatchet against the bony armor that covered that frightful carcass; but for all the damage he inflicted he might as well have struck with his open palm.

At last I could endure no longer to sit supinely by while a fellowman was dragged down to a horrible death by that repulsive reptile. Embedded in the prow of the skiff lay the spear that had been cast after me by him whom I suddenly desired to save. With a wrench I tore it loose, and standing upright in the wobbly log drove it with all the strength of my two arms straight into the gaping jaws of the hydrophidian.

With a loud hiss the creature abandoned its prey to turn upon me, but the spear, imbedded in its throat, prevented it from seizing me though it came near to overturning the skiff in its mad efforts to reach me.

CHAPTER EIGHT
The Mahar Temple

THE ABORIGINE, APPARENTLY UNINJURED, CLIMBED quickly into the skiff, and seizing the spear with me helped to hold off the infuriated creature. Blood from the wounded reptile was now crimsoning the waters about us and soon from the weakening struggles it became evident that I had inflicted a death wound upon it. Presently its efforts to reach us ceased entirely, and with a few convulsive movements it turned upon its back quite dead.

And then there came to me a sudden realization of the predicament in which I had placed myself. I was entirely within the power of the savage man whose skiff I had stolen. Still clinging to the spear I looked into his face to find him scrutinizing me intently, and there we stood for some several minutes, each clinging tenaciously to the weapon the while we gazed in stupid wonderment at each other.

What was in his mind I do not know, but in my own was merely the question as to how soon the fellow would recommence hostilities.

Presently he spoke to me, but in a tongue which I was unable to translate. I shook my head in an effort to indicate my ignorance of his language, at the same time addressing him in the bastard tongue that the Sagoths use to converse with the human slaves of the Mahars.

To my delight he understood and answered me in the same jargon.

"What do you want of my spear?" he asked.

"Only to keep you from running it through me," I replied.

"I would not do that," he said, "for you have just saved my life," and with that he released his hold upon it and squatted down in the bottom of the skiff.

"Who are you," he continued, "and from what country do you come?"

I too sat down, laying the spear between us, and tried to explain how I came to Pellucidar, and wherefrom, but it was as impossible for him to grasp or believe the strange tale I told him as I fear it is for you upon the outer crust to believe in the existence of the inner world. To him it seemed quite ridiculous to imagine that there was another world far beneath his feet peopled by beings similar to himself, and he laughed uproariously the more he thought upon it. But it was ever thus. That which has never come within the scope of our really pitifully meager world-experience cannot be—our finite minds cannot grasp that which may not exist in accordance with the conditions which obtain about us upon the outside of the insignificant grain of dust which wends its tiny way among the bowlders of the universe—the speck of moist dirt we so proudly call the World.

So I gave it up and asked him about himself. He said he was a Mezop, and that his name was Ja.

"Who are the Mezops?" I asked. "Where do they live?"

He looked at me in surprise.

"I might indeed believe that you were from another world," he said, "for who of Pellucidar could be so ignorant! The Mezops live upon the islands of the seas. In so far as I ever have heard no Mezop lives elsewhere, and no others than Mezops dwell upon islands, but of course it may be different in other far-distant lands. I do not know. At any rate in this sea and those near by it is true that only people of my race inhabit the islands.

"We are fishermen, though we be great hunters as well, often going to the mainland in search of the game that is scarce upon all but the larger islands. And we are warriors also," he added proudly. "Even the Sagoths of the Mahars fear us. Once, when Pellucidar was young, the Sagoths were wont to capture us for slaves as they do the other men of Pellucidar, it is handed down from father to son among us that this is so; but we fought so desperately and slew so many Sagoths, and those of us that were captured killed so many Mahars in their own cities that at last they learned that it were better to leave us alone, and later came the time that the Mahars became too indolent even to catch their own fish, except for amusement, and then they needed us to supply their wants, and so a truce was made between the races. Now they give us certain things which we are unable to produce in return for the fish that we catch, and the Mezops and the Mahars live in peace.

"The great ones even come to our islands. It is there, far from the prying eyes of their own Sagoths, that they practice their religious rites in the temples they have builded there with our assistance. If you live among us you will doubtless see the manner of their worship, which is strange indeed, and most unpleasant for the poor slaves they bring to take part in it."

As Ja talked I had an excellent opportunity to inspect him more closely. He was a huge fellow, standing I should say six feet six or seven inches, well developed and of a coppery red not unlike that of our own North American Indian, nor were his features dissimilar to theirs. He had the aquiline nose found among many of the higher tribes, the prominent cheek bones, and black hair and eyes, but his mouth and lips were better molded. All in all, Ja was an impressive and handsome creature, and he talked well too, even in the miserable makeshift language we were compelled to use.

During our conversation Ja had taken the paddle and was propelling the skiff with vigorous strokes toward a large island that lay some half-mile from the mainland. The skill with which he handled his crude and awkward craft elicited my deepest admiration, since it had been so short a time before that I had made such pitiful work of it.

As we touched the pretty, level beach Ja leaped out and I followed him. Together we dragged the skiff far up into the bushes that grew beyond the sand.

"We must hide our canoes," explained Ja, "for the Mezops of Luana are always at war with us and would steal them if they found them," he nodded toward an island farther out at sea, and at so great a distance that it seemed but a blur hanging in the distant sky. The upward curve of the surface of Pellucidar was constantly revealing the impossible to the surprised eyes of the outer-earthly. To see land and water curving upward in the distance until it seemed to stand on edge where it melted into the distant sky, and to feel that seas and mountains hung suspended directly above one's head required such a complete reversal of the perceptive and reasoning faculties as almost to stupefy one.

No sooner had we hidden the canoe than Ja plunged into the jungle, presently emerging into a narrow but well-defined trail which wound hither and thither much after the manner of the highways of all primitive folk, but there was one peculiarity about this Mezop trail which I was later to find distinguished them from all other trails that I ever have seen within or without the earth.

It would run on, plain and clear and well defined to end suddenly in the midst of a tangle of matted jungle, then Ja would turn directly back in his tracks for a little distance, spring into a tree, climb through it to the other side, drop onto a fallen log, leap over a low bush and alight once more upon a distinct trail which he would follow back for a short distance only to turn directly about and retrace his steps until after a mile or less this new pathway ended as suddenly and mysteriously as the former section. Then he would pass again across some media which would reveal no spoor, to take up the broken thread of the trail beyond.

As the purpose of this remarkable avenue dawned upon me I could not but admire the native shrewdness of the ancient progenitor of the Mezops who hit upon this novel plan to throw his enemies from his track and delay or thwart them in their attempts to follow him to his deep-buried cities.

To you of the outer earth it might seem a slow and tortuous method of traveling through the jungle, but were you of Pellucidar you would realize that time is no factor where time does not exist. So labyrinthine are the windings of these trails, so varied the connecting links and the distances which one must retrace one's steps from the paths' ends to find them that a Mezop often reaches man's estate before he is familiar even with those which lead from his own city to the sea.

In fact three-fourths of the education of the young male Mezop consists in familiarizing himself with these jungle avenues, and the status of an adult is largely determined by the number of trails which he can follow upon his own island. The females never learn them, since from birth to death they never leave the clearing in which the village of their nativity is situated except they be taken to mate by a male from another village, or captured in war by the enemies of their tribe.

After proceeding through the jungle for what must have been upward of five miles we emerged suddenly into a large clearing in the exact center of which stood as strange an appearing village as one might well imagine.

Large trees had been chopped down fifteen or twenty feet above the ground, and upon the tops of them spherical habitations of woven twigs, mud covered, had been built. Each ball-like house was surmounted by some manner of carven image, which Ja told me indicated the identity of the owner.

Horizontal slits, six inches high and two or three feet wide, served to admit light and ventilation. The entrances to the house were through small apertures in the bases of the trees and thence upward by rude ladders through the hollow trunks to the rooms above. The houses varied in size from two to several rooms. The largest that I entered was divided into two floors and eight apartments.

All about the village, between it and the jungle, lay beautifully cultivated fields in which the Mezops raised such cereals, fruits, and vegetables as they required. Women and children were working in these gardens as we crossed toward the village. At sight of Ja they saluted deferentially, but to me they paid not the slightest attention. Among them and about the outer verge of the cultivated area were many warriors. These too saluted Ja, by touching the points of their spears to the ground directly before them.

Ja conducted me to a large house in the center of the village—the house with eight rooms—and taking me up into it gave me food and drink. There I met his mate, a comely girl with a nursing baby in her arms. Ja told her of how I had saved his life, and she was thereafter most kind and hospitable toward me, even permitting me to hold and amuse the tiny bundle of humanity whom Ja told me would one day rule the tribe, for Ja, it seemed, was the chief of the community.

We had eaten and rested, and I had slept, much to Ja's amusement, for it seemed that he seldom if ever did so, and then the red man proposed that I accompany him to the temple of the Mahars which lay not far from his village. "We are not supposed to visit it," he said; "but the great ones cannot hear and if we keep well out of sight they need never know that we have been there. For my part I hate them and always have, but the other chieftains of the island think it best that we continue to maintain the amicable relations which exist between the two races; otherwise I should like nothing better than to lead my warriors amongst the hideous creatures and exterminate them— Pellucidar would be a better place to live were there none of them."

I wholly concurred in Ja's belief, but it seemed that it might be a difficult matter to exterminate the dominant race of Pellucidar. Thus conversing we followed the intricate trail toward the temple, which we came upon in a small clearing surrounded by enormous trees similar to those which must have flourished upon the outer crust during the carboniferous age.

Here was a mighty temple of hewn rock built in the shape of a rough oval with rounded roof in which were several large openings. No doors or windows were visible in the sides of the structure, nor was there need of any, except one entrance for the slaves, since, as Ja explained, the Mahars flew to and from their place of ceremonial, entering and leaving the building by means of the apertures in the roof.

"But," added Ja, "there is an entrance near the base of which even the Mahars know nothing. Come," and he led me across the clearing and about the end to a pile of loose rock which lay against the foot of the wall. Here he removed a couple of large bowlders, revealing a small opening which led straight within the building, or so it seemed, though as I entered after Ja I discovered myself in a narrow place of extreme darkness.

"We are within the outer wall," said Ja. "It is hollow. Follow me closely."

The red man groped ahead a few paces and then began to ascend a primitive ladder similar to that which leads from the ground to the upper stories of his house. We ascended for some forty feet when the interior of the space between the walls commenced to grow lighter and presently we came opposite an opening in the inner wall which gave us an unobstructed view of the entire interior of the temple.

The lower floor was an enormous tank of clear water in which numerous hideous Mahars swam lazily up and down. Artificial islands of granite rock dotted this artificial sea, and upon several of them I saw men and women like myself.

"What are the human beings doing here?" I asked.

"Wait and you shall see," replied Ja. "They are to take a leading part in the ceremonies which will follow the advent of the queen. You may be thankful that you are not upon the same side of the wall as they."

Scarcely had he spoken than we heard a great fluttering of wings above and a moment later a long procession of the frightful reptiles of Pellucidar winged slowly and majestically through the large central opening in the roof and circled in stately manner about the temple.

There were several Mahars first, and then at least twenty awe-inspiring pterodactyls—thipdars, they are called within Pellucidar. Behind these came the queen, flanked by other thipdars as she had been when she entered the amphitheater at Phutra.

Three times they wheeled about the interior of the oval chamber, to settle finally upon the damp, cold bowlders that fringe the outer edge of the pool. In the center of one side the largest rock was reserved for the queen, and here she took her place surrounded by her terrible guard.

All lay quiet for several minutes after settling to their places. One might have imagined them in silent prayer. The poor slaves upon the diminutive islands watched the horrid creatures with wide eyes. The men, for the most part, stood erect and stately with folded arms, awaiting their doom; but the women and children clung to one another, hiding behind the males. They are a noble-looking race, these cave men of Pellucidar, and if our progenitors were as they, the human race of the outer crust has deteriorated rather than improved with the march of the ages. All they lack is opportunity. We have opportunity, and little else.

Now the queen moved. She raised her ugly head, looking about; then very slowly she crawled to the edge of her throne and slid noiselessly into the water. Up and down the long tank she swam, turning at the ends as you have seen captive seals turn in their tiny tanks, turning upon their backs and diving below the surface.

Nearer and nearer to the island she came until at last she remained at rest before the largest, which was directly opposite her throne. Raising her hideous head from the water she fixed her great, round eyes upon the slaves. They were fat and sleek, for they had been brought from a distant Mahar city where human beings are kept in droves, and bred and fattened, as we breed and fatten beef cattle.

The queen fixed her gaze upon a plump young maiden. Her victim tried to turn away, hiding her face in her hands and kneeling behind a woman; but the reptile, with unblinking eyes, stared on with such fixity that I could have sworn her vision penetrated the woman, and the girl's arms to reach at last the very center of her brain.

Slowly the reptile's head commenced to move to and fro, but the eyes never ceased to bore toward the frightened girl, and then the victim responded. She turned wide, fear-haunted eyes toward the Mahar queen, slowly she rose to her feet, and then as though dragged by some unseen power she moved as one in a trance straight toward the reptile, her glassy eyes fixed upon those of her captor. To the water's edge she came, nor did she even pause, but stepped into the shallows beside the little island. On she moved toward the Mahar, who now slowly retreated as though leading her victim on. The water rose to the girl's knees, and still she advanced, chained by that clammy eye. Now the water was at her waist; now her armpits. Her fellows upon the island looked on in horror, helpless to avert her doom in which they saw a forecast of their own.

The Mahar sank now till only the long upper bill and eyes were exposed above the surface of the water, and the girl had advanced until the end of that repulsive beak was but an inch or two from her face, her horror-filled eyes riveted upon those of the reptile.

Now the water passed above the girl's mouth and nose—her eyes and forehead all that showed—yet still she walked on after the retreating Mahar. The queen's head slowly disappeared beneath the surface and after it went the eyes of her victim—only a slow ripple widened toward the shores to mark where the two vanished.

For a time all was silence within the temple. The slaves were motionless in terror. The Mahars watched the surface of the water for the reappearance of their queen, and presently at one end of the tank her head rose slowly into view. She was backing toward the surface, her eyes fixed before her as they had been when she dragged the helpless girl to her doom.

And then to my utter amazement I saw the forehead and eyes of the maiden come slowly out of the depths, following the gaze of the reptile just as when she had disappeared beneath the surface. On and on came the girl until she stood in water that reached barely to her knees, and though she had been beneath the surface sufficient time to have drowned her thrice over there was no indication, other than her dripping hair and glistening body, that she had been submerged at all.

Again and again the queen led the girl into the depths and out again, until the uncanny weirdness of the thing got on my nerves so that I could have leaped into the tank to the child's rescue had I not taken a firm hold of myself.

Once they were below much longer than usual, and when they came to the surface I was horrified to see that one of the girl's arms was gone—gnawed completely off at the shoulder—but the poor thing gave no indication of realizing pain, only the horror in her set eyes seemed intensified.

The next time they appeared the other arm was gone, and then the breasts, and then a part of the face—it was awful. The poor creatures on the islands awaiting their fate tried to cover their eyes with their hands to hide the fearful sight, but now I saw that they too were under the hypnotic spell of the reptiles, so that they could only crouch in terror with their eyes fixed upon the terrible thing that was transpiring before them.

Finally the queen was under much longer than ever before, and when she rose she came alone and swam sleepily toward her bowlder. The moment she mounted it seemed to be the signal for the other Mahars to enter the tank, and then commenced, upon a larger scale, a repetition of the uncanny performance through which the queen had led her victim.

Only the women and children fell prey to the Mahars—they being the weakest and most tender—and when they had satisfied their appetite for human flesh, some of them devouring two and three of the slaves, there were only a score of full-grown men left, and I thought that for some reason these were to be spared, but such was far from the case, for as the last Mahar crawled to her rock the queen's thipdars darted into the air, circled the temple once and then, hissing like steam engines, swooped down upon the remaining slaves.

There was no hypnotism here—just the plain, brutal ferocity of the beast of prey, tearing, rending, and gulping its meat, but at that it was less horrible than the uncanny method of the Mahars. By the time the thipdars had disposed of the last of the slaves the Mahars were all asleep upon their rocks, and a moment later the great pterodactyls swung back to their posts beside the queen, and themselves dropped into slumber.

"I thought the Mahars seldom, if ever, slept," I said to Ja.

"They do many things in this temple which they do not do elsewhere," he replied. "The Mahars of Phutra are not supposed to eat human flesh, yet slaves are brought here by thousands and almost always you will find Mahars on hand to consume them. I imagine that they do not bring their Sagoths here, because they are ashamed of the practice, which is supposed to obtain only among the least advanced of their race; but I would wager my canoe against a broken paddle that there is no Mahar but eats human flesh whenever she can get it."

"Why should they object to eating human flesh," I asked, "if it is true that they look upon us as lower animals?"

"It is not because they consider us their equals that they are supposed to look with abhorrence upon those who eat our flesh," replied Ja; "it is merely that we are warm-blooded animals. They would not think of eating the meat of a thag, which we consider such a delicacy, any more than I would think of eating a snake. As a matter of fact it is difficult to explain just why this sentiment should exist among them."

"I wonder if they left a single victim," I remarked, leaning far out of the opening in the rocky wall to inspect the temple better. Directly below me the water lapped the very side of the wall, there being a break in the bowlders at this point as there was at several other places about the side of the temple.

My hands were resting upon a small piece of granite which formed a part of the wall, and all my weight upon it proved too much for it. It slipped and I lunged forward. There was nothing to save myself and I plunged headforemost into the water below.

Fortunately the tank was deep at this point, and I suffered no injury from the fall, but as I was rising to the surface my mind filled with the horrors of my position as I thought of the terrible doom which awaited me the moment the eyes of the reptiles fell upon the creature that had disturbed their slumber.

As long as I could I remained beneath the surface, swimming rapidly in the direction of the islands that I might prolong my life to the utmost. At last I was forced to rise for air, and as I cast a terrified glance in the direction of the Mahars and the thipdars I was almost stunned to see that not a single one remained upon the rocks where I had last seen them, nor as I searched the temple with my eyes could I discern any within it.

For a moment I was puzzled to account for the thing, until I realized that the reptiles, being deaf, could not have been disturbed by the noise my body made when it hit the water, and that as there is no such thing as time within Pellucidar there was no telling how long I had been beneath the surface. It was a difficult thing to attempt to figure out by earthly standards—this matter of elapsed time—but when I set myself to it I began to realize that I might have been submerged a second or a month or not at all. You have no conception of the strange contradictions and impossibilities which arise when all methods of measuring time, as we know them upon earth, are non-existent.

I was about to congratulate myself upon the miracle which had saved me for the moment, when the memory of the hypnotic powers of the Mahars filled me with apprehension lest they be practicing their uncanny art upon me to the end that I merely imagined that I was alone in the temple. At the thought cold sweat broke out upon me from every pore, and as I crawled from the water onto one of the tiny islands I was trembling like a leaf—you cannot imagine the awful horror which even the simple thought of the repulsive Mahars of Pellucidar induces in the human mind, and to feel that you are in their power—that they are crawling, slimy, and abhorrent, to drag you down beneath the waters and devour you! It is frightful.

But they did not come, and at last I came to the conclusion that I was indeed alone within the temple. How long I should be alone was the next question to assail me as I swam frantically about once more in search of a means to escape.

Several times I called to Ja, but he must have left after I tumbled into the tank, for I received no response to my cries. Doubtless he had felt as certain of my doom when he saw me topple from our hiding place as I had, and lest he too should be discovered, had hastened from the temple and back to his village.

I knew that there must be some entrance to the building beside the doorways in the roof, for it did not seem reasonable to believe that the thousands of slaves which were brought here to feed the Mahars the human flesh they craved would all be carried through the air, and so I continued my search until at last it was rewarded by the discovery of several loose granite blocks in the masonry at one end of the temple.

A little effort proved sufficient to dislodge enough of these stones to permit me to crawl through into the clearing, and a moment later I had scurried across the intervening space to the dense jungle beyond.

Here I sank panting and trembling upon the matted grasses beneath the giant trees, for I felt that I had escaped from the grinning fangs of death out of the depths of my own grave. Whatever dangers lay hidden in this island jungle, there could be none so fearsome as those which I had just escaped. I knew that I could meet death bravely enough if it but came in the form of some familiar beast or man—anything other than the hideous and uncanny Mahars.

CHAPTER NINE
The Face of Death

I MUST HAVE FALLEN ASLEEP FROM EXHAUSTION. When I awoke I was very hungry, and after busying myself searching for fruit for a while, I set off through the jungle to find the beach. I knew that the island was not so large but that I could easily find the sea if I did but move in a straight line, but there came the difficulty as there was no way in which I could direct my course and hold it, the sun, of course, being always directly above my head, and the trees so thickly set that I could see no distant object which might serve to guide me in a straight line.

As it was I must have walked for a great distance since I ate four times and slept twice before I reached the sea, but at last I did so, and my pleasure at the sight of it was greatly enhanced by the chance discovery of a hidden canoe among the bushes through which I had stumbled just prior to coming upon the beach.

I can tell you that it did not take me long to pull that awkward craft down to the water and shove it far out from shore. My experience with Ja had taught me that if I were to steal another canoe I must be quick about it and get far beyond the owner's reach as soon as possible.

I must have come out upon the opposite side of the island from that at which Ja and I had entered it, for the mainland was nowhere in sight. For a long time I paddled around the shore, though well out, before I saw the mainland in the distance. At the sight of it I lost no time in directing my course toward it, for I had long since made up my mind to return to Phutra and give myself up that I might be once more with Perry and Ghak the Hairy One.

I felt that I was a fool ever to have attempted to escape alone, especially in view of the fact that our plans were already well formulated to make a break for freedom together. Of course I realized that the chances of the success of our proposed venture were slim indeed, but I knew that I never could enjoy freedom without Perry so long as the old man lived, and I had learned that the probability that I might find him was less than slight.

Had Perry been dead, I should gladly have pitted my strength and wit against the savage and primordial world in which I found myself. I could have lived in seclusion within some rocky cave until I had found the means to outfit myself with the crude weapons of the Stone Age, and then set out in search of her whose image had now become the constant companion of my waking hours, and the central and beloved figure of my dreams.

But, to the best of my knowledge, Perry still lived and it was my duty and wish to be again with him, that we might share the dangers and vicissitudes of the strange world we had discovered. And Ghak, too; the great, shaggy man had found a place in the hearts of us both, for he was indeed every inch a man and king. Uncouth, perhaps, and brutal, too, if judged too harshly by the standards of effete twentieth-century civilization, but withal noble, dignified, chivalrous, and loveable.

Chance carried me to the very beach upon which I had discovered Ja's canoe, and a short time later I was scrambling up the steep bank to retrace my steps from the plain of Phutra. But my troubles came when I entered the canyon beyond the summit, for here I found that several of them centered at the point where I crossed the divide, and which one I had traversed to reach the pass I could not for the life of me remember.

It was all a matter of chance and so I set off down that which seemed the easiest going, and in this I made the same mistake that many of us do in selecting the path along which we shall follow out the course of our lives, and again learned that it is not always best to follow the line of least resistance.

By the time I had eaten eight meals and slept twice I was convinced that I was upon the wrong trail, for between Phutra and the inland sea I had not slept at all, and had eaten but once. To retrace my steps to the summit of the divide and explore another canyon seemed the only solution of my problem, but a sudden widening and levelness of the canyon just before me seemed to suggest that it was about to open into a level country, and with the lure of discovery strong upon me I decided to proceed but a short distance farther before I turned back.

The next turn of the canyon brought me to its mouth, and before me I saw a narrow plain leading down to an ocean. At my right the side of the canyon continued to the water's edge, the valley lying to my left, and the foot of it running gradually into the sea, where it formed a broad level beach.

Clumps of strange trees dotted the landscape here and there almost to the water, and rank grass and ferns grew between. From the nature of the vegetation I was convinced that the land between the ocean and the foothills was swampy, though directly before me it seemed dry enough all the way to the sandy strip along which the restless waters advanced and retreated.

Curiosity prompted me to walk down to the beach, for the scene was very beautiful. As I passed along beside the deep and tangled vegetation of the swamp I thought that I saw a movement of the ferns at my left, but though I stopped a moment to look it was not repeated, and if anything lay hid there my eyes could not penetrate the dense foliage to discern it.

Presently I stood upon the beach looking out over the wide and lonely sea across whose forbidding bosom no human being had yet ventured, to discover what strange and mysterious lands lay beyond, or what its invisible islands held of riches, wonders, or adventure. What savage faces, what fierce and formidable beasts were this very instant watching the lapping of the waves upon its farther shore! How far did it extend? Perry had told me that the seas of Pellucidar were small in comparison with those of the outer crust, but even so this great ocean might stretch its broad expanse for thousands of miles. For countless ages it had rolled up and down its countless miles of shore, and yet today it remained all unknown beyond the tiny strip that was visible from its beaches.

The fascination of speculation was strong upon me. It was as though I had been carried back to the birth time of our own outer world to look upon its lands and seas ages before man had traversed either. Here was a new world, all untouched. It called to me to explore it. I was dreaming of the excitement and adventure which lay before us could Perry and I but escape the Mahars, when something, a slight noise I imagine, drew my attention behind me.

As I turned, romance, adventure, and discovery in the abstract took wing before the terrible embodiment of all three in concrete form that I beheld advancing upon me.

A huge, slimy amphibian it was, with toad-like body and the mighty jaws of an alligator. Its immense carcass must have weighed tons, and yet it moved swiftly and silently toward me. Upon one hand was the bluff that ran from the canyon to the sea, on the other the fearsome swamp from which the creature had sneaked upon me, behind lay the mighty untracked sea, and before me in the center of the narrow way that led to safety stood this huge mountain of terrible and menacing flesh.

A single glance at the thing was sufficient to assure me that I was facing one of those long-extinct, prehistoric creatures whose fossilized remains are found within the outer crust as far back as the Triassic formation, a gigantic labyrinthodon. And there I was, unarmed, and, with the exception of a loin cloth, as naked as I had come into the world. I could imagine how my first ancestor felt that distant, prehistoric morn that he encountered for the first time the terrifying progenitor of the thing that had me cornered now beside the restless, mysterious sea.

Unquestionably he had escaped, or I should not have been within Pellucidar or elsewhere, and I wished at that moment that he had handed down to me with the various attributes that I presumed I have inherited from him, the specific application of the instinct of self-preservation which saved him from the fate which loomed so close before me today.

To seek escape in the swamp or in the ocean would have been similar to jumping into a den of lions to escape one upon the outside. The sea and swamp both were doubtless alive with these mighty, carnivorous amphibians, and if not, the individual that menaced me would pursue me into either the sea or the swamp with equal facility.

There seemed nothing to do but stand supinely and await my end. I thought of Perry—how he would wonder what had become of me. I thought of my friends of the outer world, and of how they all would go on living their lives in total ignorance of the strange and terrible fate that had overtaken me, or unguessing the weird surroundings which had witnessed the last frightful agony of my extinction. And with these thoughts came a realization of how unimportant to the life and happiness of the world is the existence of any one of us. We may be snuffed out without an instant's warning, and for a brief day our friends speak of us with subdued voices. The following morning, while the first worm is busily engaged in testing the construction of our coffin, they are teeing up for the first hole to suffer more acute sorrow over a sliced ball than they did over our, to us, untimely demise. The labyrinthodon was coming more slowly now. He seemed to realize that escape for me was impossible, and I could have sworn that his huge, fanged jaws grinned in pleasurable appreciation of my predicament, or was it in anticipation of the juicy morsel which would so soon be pulp between those formidable teeth?

He was about fifty feet from me when I heard a voice calling to me from the direction of the bluff at my left. I looked and could have shouted in delight at the sight that met my eyes, for there stood Ja, waving frantically to me, and urging me to run for it to the cliff's base.

I had no idea that I should escape the monster that had marked me for his breakfast, but at least I should not die alone. Human eyes would watch me end. It was cold comfort I presume, but yet I derived some slight peace of mind from the contemplation of it.

To run seemed ridiculous, especially toward that steep and unscalable cliff, and yet I did so, and as I ran I saw Ja, agile as a monkey, crawl down the precipitous face of the rocks, clinging to small projections, and the tough creepers that had found root-hold here and there.

The labyrinthodon evidently thought that Ja was coming to double his portion of human flesh, so he was in no haste to pursue me to the cliff and frighten away this other tidbit. Instead he merely trotted along behind me.

As I approached the foot of the cliff I saw what Ja intended doing, but I doubted if the thing would prove successful. He had come down to within twenty feet of the bottom, and there, clinging with one hand to a small ledge, and with his feet resting precariously upon tiny bushes that grew from the solid face of the rock, he lowered the point of his long spear until it hung some six feet above the ground.

To clamber up that slim shaft without dragging Ja down and precipitating both to the same doom from which the copper-colored one was attempting to save me seemed utterly impossible, and as I came near the spear I told Ja so, and that I could not risk him to try to save myself.

But he insisted that he knew what he was doing and was in no danger himself.

"The danger is still yours," he called, "for unless you move much more rapidly than you are now, the sithic will be upon you and drag you back before ever you are halfway up the spear—he can rear up and reach you with ease anywhere below where I stand."

Well, Ja should know his own business, I thought, and so I grasped the spear and clambered up toward the red man as rapidly as I could—being so far removed from my simian ancestors as I am. I imagine the slow-witted sithic, as Ja called him, suddenly realized our intentions and that he was quite likely to lose all his meal instead of having it doubled as he had hoped.

When he saw me clambering up that spear he let out a hiss that fairly shook the ground, and came charging after me at a terrific rate. I had reached the top of the spear by this time, or almost; another six inches would give me a hold on Ja's hand, when I felt a sudden wrench from below and glancing fearfully downward saw the mighty jaws of the monster close on the sharp point of the weapon.

I made a frantic effort to reach Ja's hand, the sithic gave a tremendous tug that came near to jerking Ja from his frail hold on the surface of the rock, the spear slipped from his fingers, and still clinging to it I plunged feet foremost toward my executioner.

At the instant that he felt the spear come away from Ja's hand the creature must have opened his huge jaws to catch me, for when I came down, still clinging to the butt end of the weapon, the point yet rested in his mouth and the result was that the sharpened end transfixed his lower jaw.

With the pain he snapped his mouth closed. I fell upon his snout, lost my hold upon the spear, rolled the length of his face and head, across his short neck onto his broad back and from there to the ground.

Scarce had I touched the earth than I was upon my feet, dashing madly for the path by which I had entered this horrible valley. A glance over my shoulder showed me the sithic engaged in pawing at the spear stuck through his lower jaw, and so busily engaged did he remain in this occupation that I had gained the safety of the cliff top before he was ready to take up the pursuit. When he did not discover me in sight within the valley he dashed, hissing, into the rank vegetation of the swamp and that was the last I saw of him.

CHAPTER TEN
Phutra Again

I HASTENED TO THE CLIFF EDGE ABOVE JA AND helped him to a secure footing. He would not listen to any thanks for his attempt to save me, which had come so near miscarrying.

"I had given you up for lost when you tumbled into the Mahar temple," he said, "for not even I could save you from their clutches, and you may imagine my surprise when on seeing a canoe dragged up upon the beach of the mainland I discovered your own footprints in the sand beside it.

"I immediately set out in search of you, knowing as I did that you must be entirely unarmed and defenseless against the many dangers which lurk upon the mainland both in the form of savage beasts and reptiles, and men as well. I had no difficulty in tracking you to this point. It is well that I arrived when I did."

"But why did you do it?" I asked, puzzled at this show of friendship on the part of a man of another world and a different race and color.

"You saved my life," he replied; "from that moment it became my duty to protect and befriend you. I would have been no true Mezop had I evaded my plain duty; but it was a pleasure in this instance for I like you. I wish that you would come and live with me. You shall become a member of my tribe. Among us there is the best of hunting and fishing, and you shall have, to choose a mate from, the most beautiful girls of Pellucidar. Will you come?"

I told him about Perry then, and Dian the Beautiful, and how my duty was to them first. Afterward I should return and visit him—if I could ever find his island.

"Oh, that is easy, my friend," he said. "You need merely to come to the foot of the highest peak of the Mountains of the Clouds. There you will find a river which flows into the Lural Az. Directly opposite the mouth of the river you will see three large islands far out, so far that they are barely discernible, the one to the extreme left as you face them from the mouth of the river is Anoroc, where I rule the tribe of Anoroc."

"But how am I to find the Mountains of the Clouds?" I asked. "Men say that they are visible from half Pellucidar," he replied.

"How large is Pellucidar?" I asked, wondering what sort of theory these primitive men had concerning the form and substance of their world.

"The Mahars say it is round, like the inside of a tola shell," he answered, "but that is ridiculous, since, were it true, we should fall back were we to travel far in any direction, and all the waters of Pellucidar would run to one spot and drown us. No, Pellucidar is quite flat and extends no man knows how far in all directions. At the edges, so my ancestors have reported and handed down to me, is a great wall that prevents the earth and waters from escaping over into the burning sea whereon Pellucidar floats; but I never have been so far from Anoroc as to have seen this wall with my own eyes. However, it is quite reasonable to believe that this is true, whereas there is no reason at all in the foolish belief of the Mahars. According to them Pellucidarians who live upon the opposite side walk always with their heads pointed downward!" and Ja laughed uproariously at the very thought.

It was plain to see that the human folk of this inner world had not advanced far in learning, and the thought that the ugly Mahars had so outstripped them was a very pathetic one indeed. I wondered how many ages it would take to lift these people out of their ignorance even were it given to Perry and me to attempt it. Possibly we would be killed for our pains as were those men of the outer world who dared challenge the dense ignorance and superstitions of the earth's younger days. But it was worth the effort if the opportunity ever presented itself.

And then it occurred to me that here was an opportunity—that I might make a small beginning upon Ja, who was my friend, and thus note the effect of my teaching upon a Pellucidarian.

"Ja," I said, "what would you say were I to tell you that in so far as the Mahars' theory of the shape of Pellucidar is concerned it is correct?"

"I would say," he replied, "that either you are a fool, or took me for one."

"But, Ja," I insisted, "if their theory is incorrect how do you account for the fact that I was able to pass through the earth from the outer crust to Pellucidar. If your theory is correct all is a sea of flame beneath us, wherein no peoples could exist, and yet I come from a great world that is covered with human beings, and beasts, and birds, and fishes in mighty oceans."

"You live upon the under side of Pellucidar, and walk always with your head pointed downward?" he scoffed. "And were I to believe that, my friend, I should indeed be mad."

I attempted to explain the force of gravity to him, and by the means of the dropped fruit to illustrate how impossible it would be for a body to fall off the earth under any circumstances. He listened so intently that I thought I had made an impression, and started the train of thought that would lead him to a partial understanding of the truth. But I was mistaken.

"Your own illustration," he said finally, "proves the falsity of your theory." He dropped a fruit from his hand to the ground. "See," he said, "without support even this tiny fruit falls until it strikes something that stops it. If Pellucidar were not supported upon the flaming sea it too would fall as the fruit falls—you have proven it yourself!" He had me, that time—you could see it in his eye.

It seemed a hopeless job and I gave it up, temporarily at least, for when I contemplated the necessity explanation of our solar system and the universe I realized how futile it would be to attempt to picture to Ja or any other Pellucidarian the sun, the moon, the planets, and the countless stars. Those born within the inner world could no more conceive of such things than can we of the outer crust reduce to factors appreciable to our finite minds such terms as space and eternity.

"Well, Ja," I laughed, "whether we be walking with our feet up or down, here we are, and the question of greatest importance is not so much where we came from as where we are going now. For my part I wish that you could guide me to Phutra where I may give myself up to the Mahars once more that my friends and I may work out the plan of escape which the Sagoths interrupted when they gathered us together and drove us to the arena to witness the punishment of the slaves who killed the guardsman. I wish now that I had not left the arena for by this time my friends and I might have made good our escape, whereas this delay may mean the wrecking of all our plans, which depended for their consummation upon the continued sleep of the three Mahars who lay in the pit beneath the building in which we were confined."

"You would return to captivity?" cried Ja.

"My friends are there," I replied, "the only friends I have in Pellucidar, except yourself. What else may I do under the circumstances?"

He thought for a moment in silence. Then he shook his head sorrowfully.

"It is what a brave man and a good friend should do," he said; "yet it seems most foolish, for the Mahars will most certainly condemn you to death for running away, and so you will be accomplishing nothing for your friends by returning. Never in all my life have I heard of a prisoner returning to the Mahars of his own free will. There are but few who escape them, though some do, and these would rather die than be recaptured."

"I see no other way, Ja," I said, "though I can assure you that I would rather go to Sheol after Perry than to Phutra. However, Perry is much too pious to make the probability at all great that I should ever be called upon to rescue him from the former locality."

Ja asked me what Sheol was, and when I explained, as best I could, he said, "You are speaking of Molop Az, the flaming sea upon which Pellucidar floats. All the dead who are buried in the ground go there. Piece by piece they are carried down to Molop Az by the little demons who dwell there. We know this because when graves are opened we find that the bodies have been partially or entirely borne off. That is why we of Anoroc place our dead in high trees where the birds may find them and bear them bit by bit to the Dead World above the Land of Awful Shadow. If we kill an enemy we place his body in the ground that it may go to Molop Az."

As we talked we had been walking up the canyon down which I had come to the great ocean and the sithic. Ja did his best to dissuade me from returning to Phutra, but when he saw that I was determined to do so, he consented to guide me to a point from which I could see the plain where lay the city. To my surprise the distance was but short from the beach where I had again met Ja. It was evident that I had spent much time following the windings of a tortuous canyon, while just beyond the ridge lay the city of Phutra near to which I must have come several times.

As we topped the ridge and saw the granite gate towers dotting the flowered plain at our feet Ja made a final effort to persuade me to abandon my mad purpose and return with him to Anoroc, but I was firm in my resolve, and at last he bid me good-bye, assured in his own mind that he was looking upon me for the last time.

I was sorry to part with Ja, for I had come to like him very much indeed. With his hidden city upon the island of Anoroc as a base, and his savage warriors as escort Perry and I could have accomplished much in the line of exploration, and I hoped that were we successful in our effort to escape we might return to Anoroc later.

There was, however, one great thing to be accomplished first—at least it was the great thing to me—the finding of Dian the Beautiful. I wanted to make amends for the affront I had put upon her in my ignorance, and I wanted to—well, I wanted to see her again, and to be with her.

Down the hillside I made my way into the gorgeous field of flowers, and then across the rolling land toward the shadowless columns that guard the ways to buried Phutra. At a quarter-mile from the nearest entrance I was discovered by the Sagoth guard, and in an instant four of the gorilla-men were dashing toward me.

Though they brandished their long spears and yelled like wild Comanches I paid not the slightest attention to them, walking quietly toward them as though unaware of their existence. My manner had the effect upon them that I had hoped, and as we came quite near together they ceased their savage shouting. It was evident that they had expected me to turn and flee at sight of them, thus presenting that which they most enjoyed, a moving human target at which to cast their spears.

"What do you here?" shouted one, and then as he recognized me, "Ho! It is the slave who claims to be from another world—

he who escaped when the thag ran amuck within the amphitheater. But why do you return, having once made good your escape?"

"I did not 'escape'," I replied. "I but ran away to avoid the thag, as did others, and coming into a long passage I became confused and lost my way in the foothills beyond Phutra. Only now have I found my way back."

"And you come of your free will back to Phutra!" exclaimed one of the guardsmen.

"Where else might I go?" I asked. "I am a stranger within Pellucidar and know no other where than Phutra. Why should I not desire to be in Phutra? Am I not well fed and well treated? Am I not happy? What better lot could man desire?"

The Sagoths scratched their heads. This was a new one on them, and so being stupid brutes they took me to their masters whom they felt would be better fitted to solve the riddle of my return, for riddle they still considered it.

I had spoken to the Sagoths as I had for the purpose of throwing them off the scent of my purposed attempt at escape. If they thought that I was so satisfied with my lot within Phutra that I would voluntarily return when I had once had so excellent an opportunity to escape, they would never for an instant imagine that I could be occupied in arranging another escape immediately upon my return to the city.

So they led me before a slimy Mahar who clung to a slimy rock within the large room that was the thing's office. With cold, reptilian eyes the creature seemed to bore through the thin veneer of my deceit and read my inmost thoughts. It heeded the story which the Sagoths told of my return to Phutra, watching the gorilla-men's lips and fingers during the recital. Then it questioned me through one of the Sagoths.

"You say that you returned to Phutra of your own free will, because you think yourself better off here than elsewhere—do you not know that you may be the next chosen to give up your life in the interests of the wonderful scientific investigations that our learned ones are continually occupied with?"

I hadn't heard of anything of that nature, but I thought best not to admit it.

"I could be in no more danger here," I said, "than naked and unarmed in the savage jungles or upon the lonely plains of Pellucidar. I was fortunate, I think, to return to Phutra at all. As it was I barely escaped death within the jaws of a huge sithic. No, I am sure that I am safer in the hands of intelligent creatures such as rule Phutra. At least such would be the case in my own world, where human beings like myself rule supreme. There the higher races of man extend protection and hospitality to the stranger within their gates, and being a stranger here I naturally assumed that a like courtesy would be accorded me."

The Mahar looked at me in silence for some time after I ceased speaking and the Sagoth had translated my words to his master. The creature seemed deep in thought. Presently he communicated some message to the Sagoth. The latter turned, and motioning me to follow him, left the presence of the reptile. Behind and on either side of me marched the balance of the guard.

"What are they going to do with me?" I asked the fellow at my right.

"You are to appear before the learned ones who will question you regarding this strange world from which you say you come."

After a moment's silence he turned to me again.

"Do you happen to know," he asked, "what the Mahars do to slaves who lie to them?"

"No," I replied, "nor does it interest me, as I have no intention of lying to the Mahars."

"Then be careful that you don't repeat the impossible tale you told Sol-to-to just now—another world, indeed, where human beings rule!" he concluded in fine scorn.

"But it is the truth," I insisted. "From where else then did I come? I am not of Pellucidar. Anyone with half an eye could see that."

"It is your misfortune then," he remarked dryly, "that you may not be judged by one with but half an eye."

"What will they do with me," I asked, "if they do not have a mind to believe me?"

"You may be sentenced to the arena, or go to the pits to be used in research work by the learned ones," he replied.

"And what will they do with me there?" I persisted.

"No one knows except the Mahars and those who go to the pits with them, but as the latter never return, their knowledge does them but little good. It is said that the learned ones cut up their subjects while they are yet alive, thus learning many useful things. However I should not imagine that it would prove very useful to him who was being cut up; but of course this is all but conjecture. The chances are that ere long you will know much more about it than I," and he grinned as he spoke. The Sagoths have a well-developed sense of humor.

"And suppose it is the arena," I continued; "what then?"

"You saw the two who met the tarag and the thag the time that you escaped?" he said.

"Yes."

"Your end in the arena would be similar to what was intended for them," he explained, "though of course the same kinds of animals might not be employed."

"It is sure death in either event?" I asked.

"What becomes of those who go below with the learned ones I do not know, nor does any other," he replied; "but those who go to the arena may come out alive and thus regain their liberty, as did the two whom you saw."

"They gained their liberty? And how?"

"It is the custom of the Mahars to liberate those who remain alive within the arena after the beasts depart or are killed. Thus it has happened that several mighty warriors from far distant lands, whom we have captured on our slave raids, have battled the brutes turned in upon them and slain them, thereby winning their freedom. In the instance which you witnessed the beasts killed each other, but the result was the same—the man and woman were liberated, furnished with weapons, and started on their homeward journey. Upon the left shoulder of each a mark was burned—the mark of the Mahars—which will forever protect these two from slaving parties."

"There is a slender chance for me then if I be sent to the arena, and none at all if the learned ones drag me to the pits?"

"You are quite right," he replied; "but do not felicitate yourself too quickly should you be sent to the arena, for there is scarce one in a thousand who comes out alive."

To my surprise they returned me to the same building in which I had been confined with Perry and Ghak before my escape. At the doorway I was turned over to the guards there.

"He will doubtless be called before the investigators shortly," said he who had brought me back, "so have him in readiness."

The guards in whose hands I now found myself, upon hearing that I had returned of my own volition to Phutra evidently felt that it would be safe to give me liberty within the building as had been the custom before I had escaped, and so I was told to return to whatever duty had been mine formerly.

My first act was to hunt up Perry, whom I found poring as usual over the great tomes that he was supposed to be merely dusting and rearranging upon new shelves.

As I entered the room he glanced up and nodded pleasantly to me, only to resume his work as though I had never been away at all. I was both astonished and hurt at his indifference. And to think that I was risking death to return to him purely from a sense of duty and affection!

"Why, Perry!" I exclaimed, "haven't you a word for me after my long absence?"

"Long absence!" he repeated in evident astonishment. "What do you mean?"

"Are you crazy, Perry? Do you mean to say that you have not missed me since that time we were separated by the charging thag within the arena?"

"'That time'," he repeated. "Why man, I have but just returned from the arena! You reached here almost as soon as I.

Had you been much later I should indeed have been worried, and as it is I had intended asking you about how you escaped the beast as soon as I had completed the translation of this most interesting passage."

"Perry, you ARE mad," I exclaimed. "Why, the Lord only knows how long I have been away. I have been to other lands, discovered a new race of humans within Pellucidar, seen the Mahars at their worship in their hidden temple, and barely escaped with my life from them and from a great labyrinthodon that I met afterward, following my long and tedious wanderings across an unknown world. I must have been away for months, Perry, and now you barely look up from your work when I return and insist that we have been separated but a moment. Is that any way to treat a friend? I'm surprised at you, Perry, and if I'd thought for a moment that you cared no more for me than this I should not have returned to chance death at the hands of the Mahars for your sake."

The old man looked at me for a long time before he spoke. There was a puzzled expression upon his wrinkled face, and a look of hurt sorrow in his eyes.

"David, my boy," he said, "how could you for a moment doubt my love for you? There is something strange here that I cannot understand. I know that I am not mad, and I am equally sure that you are not; but how in the world are we to account for the strange hallucinations that each of us seems to harbor relative to the passage of time since last we saw each other. You are positive that months have gone by, while to me it seems equally certain that not more than an hour ago I sat beside you in the amphitheater. Can it be that both of us are right and at the same time both are wrong? First tell me what time is, and then maybe I can solve our problem. Do you catch my meaning?"

I didn't and said so.

"Yes," continued the old man, "we are both right. To me, bent over my book here, there has been no lapse of time. I have done little or nothing to waste my energies and so have required neither food nor sleep, but you, on the contrary, have walked and fought and wasted strength and tissue which must needs be rebuilt by nutriment and food, and so, having eaten and slept many times since last you saw me you naturally measure the lapse of time largely by these acts. As a matter of fact, David, I am rapidly coming to the conviction that there is no such thing as time—surely there can be no time here within Pellucidar, where there are no means for measuring or recording time. Why, the Mahars themselves take no account of such a thing as time. I find here in all their literary works but a single tense, the present. There seems to be neither past nor future with them. Of course it is impossible for our outer-earthly minds to grasp such a condition, but our recent experiences seem to demonstrate its existence."

It was too big a subject for me, and I said so, but Perry seemed to enjoy nothing better than speculating upon it, and after listening with interest to my account of the adventures through which I had passed he returned once more to the subject, which he was enlarging upon with considerable fluency when he was interrupted by the entrance of a Sagoth.

"Come!" commanded the intruder, beckoning to me. "The investigators would speak with you."

"Good-bye, Perry!" I said, clasping the old man's hand. "There may be nothing but the present and no such thing as time, but I feel that I am about to take a trip into the hereafter from which I shall never return. If you and Ghak should manage to escape I want you to promise me that you will find Dian the Beautiful and tell her that with my last words I asked her forgiveness for the unintentional affront I put upon her, and that my one wish was to be spared long enough to right the wrong that I had done her."

Tears came to Perry's eyes.

"I cannot believe but that you will return, David," he said. "It would be awful to think of living out the balance of my life without you among these hateful and repulsive creatures. If you are taken away I shall never escape, for I feel that I am as well off here as I should be anywhere within this buried world. Good-bye, my boy, good-bye!" and then his old voice faltered and broke, and as he hid his face in his hands the Sagoth guardsman grasped me roughly by the shoulder and hustled me from the chamber.

CHAPTER ELEVEN
Four Dead Mahars

A MOMENT LATER I WAS STANDING BEFORE A DOZEN Mahars—the social investigators of Phutra. They asked me many questions, through a Sagoth interpreter. I answered them all truthfully. They seemed particularly interested in my account of the outer earth and the strange vehicle which had brought Perry and me to Pellucidar. I thought that I had convinced them, and after they had sat in silence for a long time following my examination, I expected to be ordered returned to my quarters.

During this apparent silence they were debating through the medium of strange, unspoken language the merits of my tale. At last the head of the tribunal communicated the result of their conference to the officer in charge of the Sagoth guard.

"Come," he said to me, "you are sentenced to the experimental pits for having dared to insult the intelligence of the mighty ones with the ridiculous tale you have had the temerity to unfold to them."

"Do you mean that they do not believe me?" I asked, totally astonished.

"Believe you!" he laughed. "Do you mean to say that you expected any one to believe so impossible a lie?"

It was hopeless, and so I walked in silence beside my guard down through the dark corridors and runways toward my awful doom. At a low level we came upon a number of lighted chambers in which we saw many Mahars engaged in various occupations. To one of these chambers my guard escorted me, and before leaving they chained me to a side wall. There were other humans similarly chained. Upon a long table lay a victim even as I was ushered into the room. Several Mahars stood about the poor creature holding him down so that he could not move. Another, grasping a sharp knife with her three-toed fore foot, was laying open the victim's chest and abdomen. No anesthetic had been administered and the shrieks and groans of the tortured man were terrible to hear. This, indeed, was vivisection with a vengeance. Cold sweat broke out upon me as I realized that soon my turn would come. And to think that where there was no such thing as time I might easily imagine that my suffering was enduring for months before death finally released me!

The Mahars had paid not the slightest attention to me as I had been brought into the room. So deeply immersed were they in their work that I am sure they did not even know that the Sagoths had entered with me. The door was close by. Would that I could reach it! But those heavy chains precluded any such possibility. I looked about for some means of escape from my bonds. Upon the floor between me and the Mahars lay a tiny surgical instrument which one of them must have dropped. It looked not unlike a button-hook, but was much smaller, and its point was sharpened. A hundred times in my boyhood days had I picked locks with a buttonhook. Could I but reach that little bit of polished steel I might yet effect at least a temporary escape.

Crawling to the limit of my chain, I found that by reaching one hand as far out as I could my fingers still fell an inch short of the coveted instrument. It was tantalizing! Stretch every fiber of my being as I would, I could not quite make it.

At last I turned about and extended one foot toward the object. My heart came to my throat! I could just touch the thing! But suppose that in my effort to drag it toward me I should accidentally shove it still farther away and thus entirely out of reach! Cold sweat broke out upon me from every pore. Slowly and cautiously I made the effort. My toes dropped upon the cold metal. Gradually I worked it toward me until I felt that it was within reach of my hand and a moment later I had turned about and the precious thing was in my grasp.

Assiduously I fell to work upon the Mahar lock that held my chain. It was pitifully simple. A child might have picked it, and a moment later I was free. The Mahars were now evidently completing their work at the table. One already turned away and was examining other victims, evidently with the intention of selecting the next subject.

Those at the table had their backs toward me. But for the creature walking toward us I might have escaped that moment. Slowly the thing approached me, when its attention was attracted by a huge slave chained a few yards to my right. Here the reptile stopped and commenced to go over the poor devil carefully, and as it did so its back turned toward me for an instant, and in that instant I gave two mighty leaps that carried me out of the chamber into the corridor beyond, down which I raced with all the speed I could command.

Where I was, or whither I was going, I knew not. My only thought was to place as much distance as possible between me and that frightful chamber of torture.

Presently I reduced my speed to a brisk walk, and later realizing the danger of running into some new predicament, were I not careful, I moved still more slowly and cautiously. After a time I came to a passage that seemed in some mysterious way familiar to me, and presently, chancing to glance within a chamber which led from the corridor I saw three Mahars curled up in slumber upon a bed of skins. I could have shouted aloud in joy and relief. It was the same corridor and the same Mahars that I had intended to have lead so important a role in our escape from Phutra. Providence had indeed been kind to me, for the reptiles still slept.

My one great danger now lay in returning to the upper levels in search of Perry and Ghak, but there was nothing else to be done, and so I hastened upward. When I came to the frequented portions of the building, I found a large burden of skins in a corner and these I lifted to my head, carrying them in such a way that ends and corners fell down about my shoulders completely hiding my face. Thus disguised I found Perry and Ghak together in the chamber where we had been wont to eat and sleep.

Both were glad to see me, it was needless to say, though of course they had known nothing of the fate that had been meted out to me by my judges. It was decided that no time should now be lost before attempting to put our plan of escape to the test, as I could not hope to remain hidden from the Sagoths long, nor could I forever carry that bale of skins about upon my head without arousing suspicion. However it seemed likely that it would carry me once more safely through the crowded passages and chambers of the upper levels, and so I set out with Perry and Ghak—the stench of the illy cured pelts fairly choking me.

Together we repaired to the first tier of corridors beneath the main floor of the buildings, and here Perry and Ghak halted to await me. The buildings are cut out of the solid limestone formation. There is nothing at all remarkable about their architecture. The rooms are sometimes rectangular, sometimes circular, and again oval in shape. The corridors which connect them are narrow and not always straight. The chambers are lighted by diffused sunlight reflected through tubes similar to those by which the avenues are lighted. The lower the tiers of chambers, the darker. Most of the corridors are entirely unlighted. The Mahars can see quite well in semidarkness.

Down to the main floor we encountered many Mahars, Sagoths, and slaves; but no attention was paid to us as we had become a part of the domestic life of the building. There was but a single entrance leading from the place into the avenue and this was well guarded by Sagoths—this doorway alone were we forbidden to pass. It is true that we were not supposed to enter the deeper corridors and apartments except on special occasions when we were instructed to do so; but as we were considered a lower order without intelligence there was little reason to fear that we could accomplish any harm by so doing, and so we were not hindered as we entered the corridor which led below.

Wrapped in a skin I carried three swords, and the two bows, and the arrows which Perry and I had fashioned. As many slaves bore skin-wrapped burdens to and fro my load attracted no comment. Where I left Ghak and Perry there were no other creatures in sight, and so I withdrew one sword from the package, and leaving the balance of the weapons with Perry, started on alone toward the lower levels.

Having come to the apartment in which the three Mahars slept I entered silently on tiptoe, forgetting that the creatures were without the sense of hearing. With a quick thrust through the heart I disposed of the first but my second thrust was not so fortunate, so that before I could kill the next of my victims it had hurled itself against the third, who sprang quickly up, facing me with wide-distended jaws. But fighting is not the occupation which the race of Mahars loves, and when the thing saw that I already had dispatched two of its companions, and that my sword was red with their blood, it made a dash to escape me. But I was too quick for it, and so, half hopping, half flying, it scurried down another corridor with me close upon its heels.

Its escape meant the utter ruin of our plan, and in all probability my instant death. This thought lent wings to my feet; but even at my best I could do no more than hold my own with the leaping thing before me.

Of a sudden it turned into an apartment on the right of the corridor, and an instant later as I rushed in I found myself facing two of the Mahars. The one who had been there when we entered had been occupied with a number of metal vessels, into which had been put powders and liquids as I judged from the array of flasks standing about upon the bench where it had been working. In an instant I realized what I had stumbled upon. It was the very room for the finding of which Perry had given me minute directions. It was the buried chamber in which was hidden the Great Secret of the race of Mahars. And on the bench beside the flasks lay the skin-bound book which held the only copy of the thing I was to have sought, after dispatching the three Mahars in their sleep.

There was no exit from the room other than the doorway in which I now stood facing the two frightful reptiles. Cornered, I knew that they would fight like demons, and they were well equipped to fight if fight they must. Together they launched themselves upon me, and though I ran one of them through the heart on the instant, the other fastened its gleaming fangs about my sword arm above the elbow, and then with her sharp talons commenced to rake me about the body, evidently intent upon disemboweling me. I saw that it was useless to hope that I might release my arm from that powerful, viselike grip which seemed to be severing my arm from my body. The pain I suffered was intense, but it only served to spur me to greater efforts to overcome my antagonist

Back and forth across the floor we struggled—the Mahar dealing me terrific, cutting blows with her fore feet, while I attempted to protect my body with my left hand, at the same time watching for an opportunity to transfer my blade from my now useless sword hand to its rapidly weakening mate. At last I was successful, and with what seemed to me my last ounce of strength I ran the blade through the ugly body of my foe.

Soundless, as it had fought, it died, and though weak from pain and loss of blood, it was with an emotion of triumphant pride that I stepped across its convulsively stiffening corpse to snatch up the most potent secret of a world. A single glance assured me it was the very thing that Perry had described to me.

And as I grasped it did I think of what it meant to the human race of Pellucidar—did there flash through my mind the thought that countless generations of my own kind yet unborn would have reason to worship me for the thing that I had accomplished for them? I did not. I thought of a beautiful oval face, gazing out of limpid eyes, through a waving mass of jet-black hair. I thought of red, red lips, God-made for kissing. And of a sudden, apropos of nothing, standing there alone in the secret chamber of the Mahars of Pellucidar, I realized that I loved Dian the Beautiful.

CHAPTER TWELVE
Pursuit

FOR AN INSTANT I STOOD THERE THINKING OF HER, and then, with a sigh, I tucked the book in the thong that supported my loin cloth, and turned to leave the apartment. At the bottom of the corridor which leads aloft from the lower chambers I whistled in accordance with the prearranged signal which was to announce to Perry and Ghak that I had been successful. A moment later they stood beside me, and to my surprise I saw that Hooja the Sly One accompanied them.

"He joined us," explained Perry, "and would not be denied. The fellow is a fox. He scents escape, and rather than be thwarted of our chance now I told him that I would bring him to you, and let you decide whether he might accompany us."

I had no love for Hooja, and no confidence in him. I was sure that if he thought it would profit him he would betray us; but I saw no way out of it now, and the fact that I had killed four Mahars instead of only the three I had expected to, made it possible to include the fellow in our scheme of escape.

"Very well," I said, "you may come with us, Hooja; but at the first intimation of treachery I shall run my sword through you. Do you understand?"

He said that he did.

Some time later we had removed the skins from the four Mahars, and so succeeded in crawling inside of them ourselves that there seemed an excellent chance for us to pass unnoticed from Phutra. It was not an easy thing to fasten the hides together where we had split them along the belly to remove them from their carcasses, but by remaining out until the others had all been sewed in with my help, and then leaving an aperture in the breast of Perry's skin through which he could pass his hands to sew me up, we were enabled to accomplish our design to really much better purpose than I had hoped. We managed to keep the heads erect by passing our swords up through the necks, and by the same means were enabled to move them about in a life-like manner. We had our greatest difficulty with the webbed feet, but even that problem was finally solved, so that when we moved about we did so quite naturally. Tiny holes punctured in the baggy throats into which our heads were thrust permitted us to see well enough to guide our progress.

Thus we started up toward the main floor of the building. Ghak headed the strange procession, then came Perry, followed by Hooja, while I brought up the rear, after admonishing Hooja that I had so arranged my sword that I could thrust it through the head of my disguise into his vitals were he to show any indication of faltering.

As the noise of hurrying feet warned me that we were entering the busy corridors of the main level, my heart came up into my mouth. It is with no sense of shame that I admit that I was frightened—never before in my life, nor since, did I experience any such agony of soulsearing fear and suspense as enveloped me. If it be possible to sweat blood, I sweat it then.

Slowly, after the manner of locomotion habitual to the Mahars, when they are not using their wings, we crept through throngs of busy slaves, Sagoths, and Mahars. After what seemed an eternity we reached the outer door which leads into the main avenue of Phutra. Many Sagoths loitered near the opening. They glanced at Ghak as he padded between them. Then Perry passed, and then Hooja. Now it was my turn, and then in a sudden fit of freezing terror I realized that the warm blood from my wounded arm was trickling down through the dead foot of the Mahar skin I wore and leaving its tell-tale mark upon the pavement, for I saw a Sagoth call a companion's attention to it.

The guard stepped before me and pointing to my bleeding foot spoke to me in the sign language which these two races employ as a means of communication. Even had I known what he was saying I could not have replied with the dead thing that covered me. I once had seen a great Mahar freeze a presumptuous Sagoth with a look. It seemed my only hope, and so I tried it. Stopping in my tracks I moved my sword so that it made the dead head appear to turn inquiring eyes upon the gorilla-man. For a long moment I stood perfectly still, eyeing the fellow with those dead eyes. Then I lowered the head and started slowly on. For a moment all hung in the balance, but before I touched him the guard stepped to one side, and I passed on out into the avenue.

On we went up the broad street, but now we were safe for the very numbers of our enemies that surrounded us on all sides. Fortunately, there was a great concourse of Mahars repairing to the shallow lake which lies a mile or more from the city. They go there to indulge their amphibian proclivities in diving for small fish, and enjoying the cool depths of the water. It is a fresh-water lake, shallow, and free from the larger reptiles which make the use of the great seas of Pellucidar impossible for any but their own kind.

In the thick of the crowd we passed up the steps and out onto the plain. For some distance Ghak remained with the stream that was traveling toward the lake, but finally, at the bottom of a little gully he halted, and there we remained until all had passed and we were alone. Then, still in our disguises, we set off directly away from Phutra.

The heat of the vertical rays of the sun was fast making our horrible prisons unbearable, so that after passing a low divide, and entering a sheltering forest, we finally discarded the Mahar skins that had brought us thus far in safety.

I shall not weary you with the details of that bitter and galling flight. How we traveled at a dogged run until we dropped in our tracks. How we were beset by strange and terrible beasts. How we barely escaped the cruel fangs of lions and tigers the size of which would dwarf into pitiful insignificance the greatest felines of the outer world.

On and on we raced, our one thought to put as much distance between ourselves and Phutra as possible. Ghak was leading us to his own land—the land of Sari. No sign of pursuit had developed, and yet we were sure that somewhere behind us relentless Sagoths were dogging our tracks. Ghak said they never failed to hunt down their quarry until they had captured it or themselves been turned back by a superior force.

Our only hope, he said, lay in reaching his tribe which was quite strong enough in their mountain fastness to beat off any number of Sagoths.

At last, after what seemed months, and may, I now realize, have been years, we came in sight of the dun escarpment which buttressed the foothills of Sari. At almost the same instant, Hooja, who looked ever quite as much behind as before, announced that he could see a body of men far behind us topping a low ridge in our wake. It was the long-expected pursuit.

I asked Ghak if we could make Sari in time to escape them.

"We may," he replied; "but you will find that the Sagoths can move with incredible swiftness, and as they are almost tireless they are doubtless much fresher than we. Then…" he paused, glancing at Perry.

I knew what he meant. The old man was exhausted. For much of the period of our flight either Ghak or I had half supported him on the march. With such a handicap, less fleet pursuers than the Sagoths might easily overtake us before we could scale the rugged heights which confronted us.

"You and Hooja go on ahead," I said. "Perry and I will make it if we are able. We cannot travel as rapidly as you two, and there is no reason why all should be lost because of that. It can't be helped—we have simply to face it."

"I will not desert a companion," was Ghak's simple reply. I hadn't known that this great, hairy, primeval man had any such nobility of character stowed away inside him. I had always liked him, but now to my liking was added honor and respect. Yes, and love.

But still I urged him to go on ahead, insisting that if he could reach his people he might be able to bring out a sufficient force to drive off the Sagoths and rescue Perry and myself.

No, he wouldn't leave us, and that was all there was to it, but he suggested that Hooja might hurry on and warn the Sarians of the king's danger. It didn't require much urging to start Hooja—the naked idea was enough to send him leaping on ahead of us into the foothills which we now had reached.

Perry realized that he was jeopardizing Ghak's life and mine and the old fellow fairly begged us to go on without him, although I knew that he was suffering a perfect anguish of terror at the thought of falling into the hands of the Sagoths. Ghak finally solved the problem, in part, by lifting Perry in his powerful arms and carrying him. While the act cut down Ghak's speed he still could travel faster thus than when half supporting the stumbling old man.

CHAPTER THIRTEEN
The Sly One

THE SAGOTHS WERE GAINING ON US RAPIDLY, FOR once they had sighted us they had greatly increased their speed. On and on we stumbled up the narrow canyon that Ghak had chosen to approach the heights of Sari. On either side rose precipitous cliffs of gorgeous, parti-colored rock, while beneath our feet a thick mountain grass formed a soft and noiseless carpet. Since we had entered the canyon we had had no glimpse of our pursuers, and I was commencing to hope that they had lost our trail and that we would reach the now rapidly nearing cliffs in time to scale them before we should be overtaken.

Ahead we neither saw nor heard any sign which might betoken the success of Hooja's mission. By now he should have reached the outposts of the Sarians, and we should at least hear the savage cries of the tribesmen as they swarmed to arms in answer to their king's appeal for succor. In another moment the frowning cliffs ahead should be black with primeval warriors. But nothing of the kind happened—as a matter of fact the Sly One had betrayed us. At the moment that we expected to see Sarian spearmen charging to our relief at Hooja's back, the craven traitor was sneaking around the outskirts of the nearest

Sarian village, that he might come up from the other side when it was too late to save us, claiming that he had become lost among the mountains.

Hooja still harbored ill will against me because of the blow I had struck in Dian's protection, and his malevolent spirit was equal to sacrificing us all that he might be revenged upon me.

As we drew nearer the barrier cliffs and no sign of rescuing Sarians appeared Ghak became both angry and alarmed, and presently as the sound of rapidly approaching pursuit fell upon our ears, he called to me over his shoulder that we were lost.

A backward glance gave me a glimpse of the first of the Sagoths at the far end of a considerable stretch of canyon through which we had just passed, and then a sudden turning shut the ugly creature from my view; but the loud howl of triumphant rage which rose behind us was evidence that the gorilla-man had sighted us.

Again the canyon veered sharply to the left, but to the right another branch ran on at a lesser deviation from the general direction, so that appeared more like the main canyon than the lefthand branch. The Sagoths were now not over two hundred and fifty yards behind us, and I saw that it was hopeless for us to expect to escape other than by a ruse. There was a bare chance of saving Ghak and Perry, and as I reached the branching of the canyon I took the chance.

Pausing there I waited until the foremost Sagoth hove into sight. Ghak and Perry had disappeared around a bend in the left-hand canyon, and as the Sagoth's savage yell announced that he had seen me I turned and fled up the right-hand branch. My ruse was successful, and the entire party of man-hunters raced headlong after me up one canyon while Ghak bore Perry to safety up the other.

Running has never been my particular athletic forte, and now when my very life depended upon fleetness of foot I cannot say that I ran any better than on the occasions when my pitiful base running had called down upon my head the rooter's raucous and reproachful cries of "Ice Wagon," and "Call a cab."

The Sagoths were gaining on me rapidly. There was one in particular, fleeter than his fellows, who was perilously close. The canyon had become a rocky slit, rising roughly at a steep angle toward what seemed a pass between two abutting peaks. What lay beyond I could not even guess—possibly a sheer drop of hundreds of feet into the corresponding valley upon the other side. Could it be that I had plunged into a cul-de-sac?

Realizing that I could not hope to outdistance the Sagoths to the top of the canyon I had determined to risk all in an attempt to check them temporarily, and to this end had unslung my rudely made bow and plucked an arrow from the skin quiver which hung behind my shoulder. As I fitted the shaft with my right hand I stopped and wheeled toward the gorilla-man.

In the world of my birth I never had drawn a shaft, but since our escape from Phutra I had kept the party supplied with small game by means of my arrows, and so, through necessity, had developed a fair degree of accuracy. During our flight from Phutra I had restrung my bow with a piece of heavy gut taken from a huge tiger which Ghak and I had worried and finally dispatched with arrows, spear, and sword. The hard wood of the bow was extremely tough and this, with the strength and elasticity of my new string, gave me unwonted confidence in my weapon.

Never had I greater need of steady nerves than then—never were my nerves and muscles under better control. I sighted as carefully and deliberately as though at a straw target. The Sagoth had never before seen a bow and arrow, but of a sudden it must have swept over his dull intellect that the thing I held toward him was some sort of engine of destruction, for he too came to a halt, simultaneously swinging his hatchet for a throw. It is one of the many methods in which they employ this weapon, and the accuracy of aim which they achieve, even under the most unfavorable circumstances, is little short of miraculous.

My shaft was drawn back its full length—my eye had centered its sharp point upon the left breast of my adversary; and then he launched his hatchet and I released my arrow. At the instant that our missiles flew I leaped to one side, but the Sagoth sprang forward to follow up his attack with a spear thrust. I felt the swish of the hatchet as it grazed my head, and at the same instant my shaft pierced the Sagoth's savage heart, and with a single groan he lunged almost at my feet—stone dead. Close behind him were two more—fifty yards perhaps—but the distance gave me time to snatch up the dead guardsman's shield, for the close call his hatchet had just given me had borne in upon me the urgent need I had for one. Those which I had purloined at Phutra we had not been able to bring along because their size precluded our concealing them within the skins of the Mahars which had brought us safely from the city.

With the shield slipped well up on my left arm I let fly with another arrow, which brought down a second Sagoth, and then as his fellow's hatchet sped toward me I caught it upon the shield, and fitted another shaft for him; but he did not wait to receive it. Instead, he turned and retreated toward the main body of gorilla-men. Evidently he had seen enough of me for the moment.

Once more I took up my flight, nor were the Sagoths apparently overanxious to press their pursuit so closely as before. Unmolested I reached the top of the canyon where I found a sheer drop of two or three hundred feet to the bottom of a rocky chasm; but on the left a narrow ledge rounded the shoulder of the overhanging cliff. Along this I advanced, and at a sudden turning, a few yards beyond the canyon's end, the path widened, and at my left I saw the opening to a large cave. Before, the ledge continued until it passed from sight about another projecting buttress of the mountain.

Here, I felt, I could defy an army, for but a single foeman could advance upon me at a time, nor could he know that I was awaiting him until he came full upon me around the corner of the turn. About me lay scattered stones crumbled from the cliff above. They were of various sizes and shapes, but enough were of handy dimensions for use as ammunition in lieu of my precious arrows. Gathering a number of stones into a little pile beside the mouth of the cave I waited the advance of the Sagoths.

As I stood there, tense and silent, listening for the first faint sound that should announce the approach of my enemies, a slight noise from within the cave's black depths attracted my attention. It might have been produced by the moving of the great body of some huge beast rising from the rock floor of its lair. At almost the same instant I thought that I caught the scraping of hide sandals upon the ledge beyond the turn. For the next few seconds my attention was considerably divided.

And then from the inky blackness at my right I saw two flaming eyes glaring into mine. They were on a level that was over two feet above my head. It is true that the beast who owned them might be standing upon a ledge within the cave, or that it might be rearing up upon its hind legs; but I had seen enough of the monsters of Pellucidar to know that I might be facing some new and frightful Titan whose dimensions and ferocity eclipsed those of any I had seen before.

Whatever it was, it was coming slowly toward the entrance of the cave, and now, deep and forbidding, it uttered a low and ominous growl. I waited no longer to dispute possession of the ledge with the thing which owned that voice. The noise had not been loud—I doubt if the Sagoths heard it at all—but the suggestion of latent possibilities behind it was such that I knew it would only emanate from a gigantic and ferocious beast.

As I backed along the ledge I soon was past the mouth of the cave, where I no longer could see those fearful flaming eyes, but an instant later I caught sight of the fiendish face of a Sagoth as it warily advanced beyond the cliff's turn on the far side of the cave's mouth. As the fellow saw me he leaped along the ledge in pursuit, and after him came as many of his companions as could crowd upon each other's heels. At the same time the beast emerged from the cave, so that he and the Sagoths came face to face upon that narrow ledge.

The thing was an enormous cave bear, rearing its colossal bulk fully eight feet at the shoulder, while from the tip of its nose to the end of its stubby tail it was fully twelve feet in length. As it sighted the Sagoths it emitted a most frightful roar, and with open mouth charged full upon them. With a cry of terror the foremost gorilla-man turned to escape, but behind him he ran full upon his on-rushing companions.

The horror of the following seconds is indescribable. The Sagoth nearest the cave bear, finding his escape blocked, turned and leaped deliberately to an awful death upon the jagged rocks three hundred feet below. Then those giant jaws reached out and gathered in the next—there was a sickening sound of crushing bones, and the mangled corpse was dropped over the cliff's edge. Nor did the mighty beast even pause in his steady advance along the ledge.

Shrieking Sagoths were now leaping madly over the precipice to escape him, and the last I saw he rounded the turn still pursuing the demoralized remnant of the man hunters. For a long time I could hear the horrid roaring of the brute intermingled with the screams and shrieks of his victims, until finally the awful sounds dwindled and disappeared in the distance.

Later I learned from Ghak, who had finally come to his tribesmen and returned with a party to rescue me, that the ryth, as it is called, pursued the Sagoths until it had exterminated the entire band. Ghak was, of course, positive that I had fallen prey to the terrible creature, which, within Pellucidar, is truly the king of beasts.

Not caring to venture back into the canyon, where I might fall prey either to the cave bear or the Sagoths I continued on along the ledge, believing that by following around the mountain I could reach the land of Sari from another direction. But I evidently became confused by the twisting and turning of the canyons and gullies, for I did not come to the land of Sari then, nor for a long time thereafter.

CHAPTER FOURTEEN
The Garden of Eden

WITH NO HEAVENLY GUIDE, IT IS LITTLE WONDER that I became confused and lost in the labyrinthine maze of those mighty hills. What, in reality, I did was to pass entirely through them and come out above the valley upon the farther side. I know that I wandered for a long time, until tired and hungry I came upon a small cave in the face of the limestone formation which had taken the place of the granite farther back.

The cave which took my fancy lay halfway up the precipitous side of a lofty cliff. The way to it was such that I knew no extremely formidable beast could frequent it, nor was it large enough to make a comfortable habitat for any but the smaller mammals or reptiles. Yet it was with the utmost caution that I crawled within its dark interior.

Here I found a rather large chamber, lighted by a narrow cleft in the rock above which let the sunlight filter in in sufficient quantities partially to dispel the utter darkness which I had expected. The cave was entirely empty, nor were there any signs of its having been recently occupied. The opening was comparatively small, so that after considerable effort I was able to lug up a bowlder from the valley below which entirely blocked it.

Then I returned again to the valley for an armful of grasses and on this trip was fortunate enough to knock over an orthopi, the diminutive horse of Pellucidar, a little animal about the size of a fox terrier, which abounds in all parts of the inner world. Thus, with food and bedding I returned to my lair, where after a meal of raw meat, to which I had now become quite accustomed, I dragged the bowlder before the entrance and curled myself upon a bed of grasses—a naked, primeval, cave man, as savagely primitive as my prehistoric progenitors.

I awoke rested but hungry, and pushing the bowlder aside crawled out upon the little rocky shelf which was my front porch. Before me spread a small but beautiful valley, through the center of which a clear and sparkling river wound its way down to an inland sea, the blue waters of which were just visible between the two mountain ranges which embraced this little paradise. The sides of the opposite hills were green with verdure, for a great forest clothed them to the foot of the red and yellow and copper green of the towering crags which formed their summit. The valley itself was carpeted with a luxuriant grass, while here and there patches of wild flowers made great splashes of vivid color against the prevailing green.

Dotted over the face of the valley were little clusters of palmlike trees—three or four together as a rule. Beneath these stood antelope, while others grazed in the open, or wandered gracefully to a nearby ford to drink. There were several species of this beautiful animal, the most magnificent somewhat resembling the giant eland of Africa, except that their spiral horns form a complete curve backward over their ears and then forward again beneath them, ending in sharp and formidable points some two feet before the face and above the eyes. In size they remind one of a pure bred Hereford bull, yet they are very agile and fast. The broad yellow bands that stripe the dark roan of their coats made me take them for zebra when I first saw them. All in all they are handsome animals, and added the finishing touch to the strange and lovely landscape that spread before my new home.

I had determined to make the cave my headquarters, and with it as a base make a systematic exploration of the surrounding country in search of the land of Sari. First I devoured the remainder of the carcass of the orthopi I had killed before my last sleep. Then I hid the Great Secret in a deep niche at the back of my cave, rolled the bowlder before my front door, and with bow, arrows, sword, and shield scrambled down into the peaceful valley.

The grazing herds moved to one side as I passed through them, the little orthopi evincing the greatest wariness and galloping to safest distances. All the animals stopped feeding as

I approached, and after moving to what they considered a safe distance stood contemplating me with serious eyes and up-cocked ears. Once one of the old bull antelopes of the striped species lowered his head and bellowed angrily—even taking a few steps in my direction, so that I thought he meant to charge; but after I had passed, he resumed feeding as though nothing had disturbed him.

Near the lower end of the valley I passed a number of tapirs, and across the river saw a great sadok, the enormous double-horned progenitor of the modern rhinoceros. At the valley's end the cliffs upon the left ran out into the sea, so that to pass around them as I desired to do it was necessary to scale them in search of a ledge along which I might continue my journey. Some fifty feet from the base I came upon a projection which formed a natural path along the face of the cliff, and this I followed out over the sea toward the cliff's end.

Here the ledge inclined rapidly upward toward the top of the cliffs—the stratum which formed it evidently having been forced up at this steep angle when the mountains behind it were born. As I climbed carefully up the ascent my attention suddenly was attracted aloft by the sound of strange hissing, and what resembled the flapping of wings.

And at the first glance there broke upon my horrified vision the most frightful thing I had seen even within Pellucidar. It was a giant dragon such as is pictured in the legends and fairy tales of earth folk. Its huge body must have measured forty feet in length, while the batlike wings that supported it in midair had a spread of fully thirty. Its gaping jaws were armed with long, sharp teeth, and its claw equipped with horrible talons.

The hissing noise which had first attracted my attention was issuing from its throat, and seemed to be directed at something beyond and below me which I could not see. The ledge upon which I stood terminated abruptly a few paces farther on, and as I reached the end I saw the cause of the reptile's agitation.

Some time in past ages an earthquake had produced a fault at this point, so that beyond the spot where I stood the strata had slipped down a matter of twenty feet. The result was that the continuation of my ledge lay twenty feet below me, where it ended as abruptly as did the end upon which I stood.

And here, evidently halted in flight by this insurmountable break in the ledge, stood the object of the creature's attack—a girl cowering upon the narrow platform, her face buried in her arms, as though to shut out the sight of the frightful death which hovered just above her.

The dragon was circling lower, and seemed about to dart in upon its prey. There was no time to be lost, scarce an instant in which to weigh the possible chances that I had against the awfully armed creature; but the sight of that frightened girl below me called out to all that was best in me, and the instinct for protection of the other sex, which nearly must have equaled the instinct of self-preservation in primeval man, drew me to the girl's side like an irresistible magnet.

Almost thoughtless of the consequences, I leaped from the end of the ledge upon which I stood, for the tiny shelf twenty feet below. At the same instant the dragon darted in toward the girl, but my sudden advent upon the scene must have startled him for he veered to one side, and then rose above us once more.

The noise I made as I landed beside her convinced the girl that the end had come, for she thought I was the dragon; but finally when no cruel fangs closed upon her she raised her eyes in astonishment. As they fell upon me the expression that came into them would be difficult to describe; but her feelings could scarcely have been one whit more complicated than my own—for the wide eyes that looked into mine were those of Dian the Beautiful.

"Dian!" I cried. "Dian! Thank God that I came in time."

"You?" she whispered, and then she hid her face again; nor could I tell whether she were glad or angry that I had come.

Once more the dragon was sweeping toward us, and so rapidly that I had no time to unsling my bow. All that I could do was to snatch up a rock, and hurl it at the thing's hideous face. Again my aim was true, and with a hiss of pain and rage the reptile wheeled once more and soared away.

Quickly I fitted an arrow now that I might be ready at the next attack, and as I did so I looked down at the girl, so that I surprised her in a surreptitious glance which she was stealing at me; but immediately, she again covered her face with her hands.

"Look at me, Dian," I pleaded. "Are you not glad to see me?"

She looked straight into my eyes.

"I hate you," she said, and then, as I was about to beg for a fair hearing she pointed over my shoulder. "The thipdar comes," she said, and I turned again to meet the reptile.

So this was a thipdar. I might have known it. The cruel bloodhound of the Mahars. The long-extinct pterodactyl of the outer world. But this time I met it with a weapon it never had faced before. I had selected my longest arrow, and with all my strength had bent the bow until the very tip of the shaft rested upon the thumb of my left hand, and then as the great creature darted toward us I let drive straight for that tough breast.

Hissing like the escape valve of a steam engine, the mighty creature fell turning and twisting into the sea below, my arrow buried completely in its carcass. I turned toward the girl. She was looking past me. It was evident that she had seen the thipdar die.

"Dian," I said, "won't you tell me that you are not sorry that I have found you?"

"I hate you," was her only reply; but I imagined that there was less vehemence in it than before—yet it might have been but my imagination.

"Why do you hate me, Dian?" I asked, but she did not answer me.

"What are you doing here?" I asked, "and what has happened to you since Hooja freed you from the Sagoths?"

At first I thought that she was going to ignore me entirely, but finally she thought better of it.

"I was again running away from Jubal the Ugly One," she said. "After I escaped from the Sagoths I made my way alone back to my own land; but on account of Jubal I did not dare enter the villages or let any of my friends know that I had returned for fear that Jubal might find out. By watching for a long time I found that my brother had not yet returned, and so I continued to live in a cave beside a valley which my race seldom frequents, awaiting the time that he should come back and free me from Jubal.

"But at last one of Jubal's hunters saw me as I was creeping toward my father's cave to see if my brother had yet returned and he gave the alarm and Jubal set out after me. He has been pursuing me across many lands. He cannot be far behind me now. When he comes he will kill you and carry me back to his cave. He is a terrible man. I have gone as far as I can go, and there is no escape," and she looked hopelessly up at the continuation of the ledge twenty feet above us.

"But he shall not have me," she suddenly cried, with great vehemence. "The sea is there…" She pointed over the edge of the cliff. "…and the sea shall have me rather than Jubal."

"But I have you now Dian," I cried; "nor shall Jubal, nor any other have you, for you are mine," and I seized her hand, nor did I lift it above her head and let it fall in token of release.

She had risen to her feet, and was looking straight into my eyes with level gaze.

"I do not believe you," she said, "for if you meant it you would have done this when the others were present to witness it—then I should truly have been your mate; now there is no one to see you do it, for you know that without witnesses your act does not bind you to me," and she withdrew her hand from mine and turned away.

I tried to convince her that I was sincere, but she simply couldn't forget the humiliation that I had put upon her on that other occasion.

"If you mean all that you say you will have ample chance to prove it," she said, "if Jubal does not catch and kill you. I am in your power, and the treatment you accord me will be the best proof of your intentions toward me. I am not your mate, and again I tell you that I hate you, and that I should be glad if I never saw you again."

Dian certainly was candid. There was no gainsaying that. In fact I found candor and directness to be quite a marked characteristic of the cave men of Pellucidar. Finally I suggested that we make some attempt to gain my cave, where we might escape the searching Jubal, for I am free to admit that I had no considerable desire to meet the formidable and ferocious creature, of whose mighty prowess Dian had told me when I first met her. He it was who, armed with a puny knife, had met and killed a cave bear in a hand-to-hand struggle. It was Jubal who could cast his spear entirely through the armored carcass of the sadok at fifty paces. It was he who had crushed the skull of a charging dyryth with a single blow of his war club. No, I was not pining to meet the Ugly One—and it was quite certain that I should not go out and hunt for him; but the matter was taken out of my hands very quickly, as is often the way, and I did meet Jubal the Ugly One face to face.

This is how it happened. I had led Dian back along the ledge the way she had come, searching for a path that would lead us to the top of the cliff, for I knew that we could then cross over to the edge of my own little valley, where I felt certain we should find a means of ingress from the cliff top. As we proceeded along the ledge I gave Dian minute directions for finding my cave against the chance of something happening to me. I knew that she would be quite safely hidden away from pursuit once she gained the shelter of my lair, and the valley would afford her ample means of sustenance.

Also, I was very much piqued by her treatment of me. My heart was sad and heavy, and I wanted to make her feel badly by suggesting that something terrible might happen to me—that I might, in fact, be killed. But it didn't work worth a cent, at least as far as I could perceive. Dian simply shrugged those magnificent shoulders of hers, and murmured something to the effect that one was not rid of trouble so easily as that.

For a while I kept still. I was utterly squelched. And to think that I had twice protected her from attack—the last time risking my life to save hers. It was incredible that even a daughter of the Stone Age could be so ungrateful—so heartless; but maybe her heart partook of the qualities of her epoch.

Presently we found a rift in the cliff which had been widened and extended by the action of the water draining through it from the plateau above. It gave us a rather rough climb to the summit, but finally we stood upon the level mesa which stretched back for several miles to the mountain range. Behind us lay the broad inland sea, curving upward in the horizonless distance to merge into the blue of the sky, so that for all the world it looked as though the sea lapped back to arch completely over us and disappear beyond the distant mountains at our backs—the weird and uncanny aspect of the seascapes of Pellucidar balk description.

At our right lay a dense forest, but to the left the country was open and clear to the plateau's farther verge. It was in this direction that our way led, and we had turned to resume our journey when Dian touched my arm. I turned to her, thinking that she was about to make peace overtures; but I was mistaken.

"Jubal," she said, and nodded toward the forest.

I looked, and there, emerging from the dense wood, came a perfect whale of a man. He must have been seven feet tall, and proportioned accordingly. He still was too far off to distinguish his features.

"Run," I said to Dian. "I can engage him until you get a good start. Maybe I can hold him until you have gotten entirely away," and then, without a backward glance, I advanced to meet the Ugly One. I had hoped that Dian would have a kind word to say to me before she went, for she must have known that I was going to my death for her sake; but she never even so much as bid me good-bye, and it was with a heavy heart that I strode through the flower-bespangled grass to my doom.

When I had come close enough to Jubal to distinguish his features I understood how it was that he had earned the sobriquet of Ugly One. Apparently some fearful beast had ripped away one entire side of his face. The eye was gone, the nose, and all the flesh, so that his jaws and all his teeth were exposed and grinning through the horrible scar.

Formerly he may have been as good to look upon as the others of his handsome race, and it may be that the terrible result of this encounter had tended to sour an already strong and brutal character. However this may be it is quite certain that he was not a pretty sight, and now that his features, or what remained of them, were distorted in rage at the sight of Dian with another male, he was indeed most terrible to see—and much more terrible to meet.

He had broken into a run now, and as he advanced he raised his mighty spear, while I halted and fitting an arrow to my bow took as steady aim as I could. I was somewhat longer than usual, for I must confess that the sight of this awful man had wrought upon my nerves to such an extent that my knees were anything but steady. What chance had I against this mighty warrior for whom even the fiercest cave bear had no terrors! Could I hope to best one who slaughtered the sadok and dyryth singlehanded! I shuddered; but, in fairness to myself, my fear was more for Dian than for my own fate.

And then the great brute launched his massive stone-tipped spear, and I raised my shield to break the force of its terrific velocity. The impact hurled me to my knees, but the shield had deflected the missile and I was unscathed. Jubal was rushing upon me now with the only remaining weapon that he carried—a murderous-looking knife. He was too close for a careful bowshot, but I let drive at him as he came, without taking aim. My arrow pierced the fleshy part of his thigh, inflicting a painful but not disabling wound. And then he was upon me.

My agility saved me for the instant. I ducked beneath his raised arm, and when he wheeled to come at me again he found a sword's point in his face. And a moment later he felt an inch or two of it in the muscles of his knife arm, so that thereafter he went more warily.

It was a duel of strategy now—the great, hairy man maneuvering to get inside my guard where he could bring those giant thews to play, while my wits were directed to the task of keeping him at arm's length. Thrice he rushed me, and thrice I caught his knife blow upon my shield. Each time my sword found his body—once penetrating to his lung. He was covered with blood by this time, and the internal hemorrhage induced paroxysms of coughing that brought the red stream through the hideous mouth and nose, covering his face and breast with bloody froth. He was a most unlovely spectacle, but he was far from dead.

As the duel continued I began to gain confidence, for, to be perfectly candid, I had not expected to survive the first rush of that monstrous engine of ungoverned rage and hatred. And I think that Jubal, from utter contempt of me, began to change to a feeling of respect, and then in his primitive mind there evidently loomed the thought that perhaps at last he had met his master, and was facing his end.

At any rate it is only upon this hypothesis that I can account for his next act, which was in the nature of a last resort—a sort of forlorn hope, which could only have been born of the belief that if he did not kill me quickly I should kill him. It happened on the occasion of his fourth charge, when, instead of striking at me with his knife, he dropped that weapon, and seizing my sword blade in both his hands wrenched the weapon from my grasp as easily as from a babe.

Flinging it far to one side he stood motionless for just an instant glaring into my face with such a horrid leer of malignant triumph as to almost unnerve me—then he sprang for me with his bare hands. But it was Jubal's day to learn new methods of warfare. For the first time he had seen a bow and arrows, never before that duel had he beheld a sword, and now he learned what a man who knows may do with his bare fists.

As he came for me, like a great bear, I ducked again beneath his outstretched arm, and as I came up planted as clean a blow upon his jaw as ever you have seen. Down went that great mountain of flesh sprawling upon the ground. He was so surprised and dazed that he lay there for several seconds before he made any attempt to rise, and I stood over him with another dose ready when he should gain his knees.

Up he came at last, almost roaring in his rage and mortification; but he didn't stay up—I let him have a left fair on the point of the jaw that sent him tumbling over on his back. By this time I think Jubal had gone mad with hate, for no sane man would have come back for more as many times as he did. Time after time I bowled him over as fast as he could stagger up, until toward the last he lay longer on the ground between blows, and each time came up weaker than before.

He was bleeding very profusely now from the wound in his lungs, and presently a terrific blow over the heart sent him reeling heavily to the ground, where he lay very still, and somehow I knew at once that Jubal the Ugly One would never get up again. But even as I looked upon that massive body lying there so grim and terrible in death, I could not believe that I, single-handed, had bested this slayer of fearful beasts—this gigantic ogre of the Stone Age.

Picking up my sword I leaned upon it, looking down on the dead body of my foeman, and as I thought of the battle I had just fought and won a great idea was born in my brain—the outcome of this and the suggestion that Perry had made within the city of Phutra. If skill and science could render a comparative pygmy the master of this mighty brute, what could not the brute's fellows accomplish with the same skill and science. Why all Pellucidar would be at their feet—and I would be their king and Dian their queen.

Dian! A little wave of doubt swept over me. It was quite within the possibilities of Dian to look down upon me even were I king. She was quite the most superior person I ever had met—with the most convincing way of letting you know that she was superior. Well, I could go to the cave, and tell her that I had killed Jubal, and then she might feel more kindly toward me, since I had freed her of her tormentor. I hoped that she had found the cave easily—it would be terrible had I lost her again, and I turned to gather up my shield and bow to hurry after her, when to my astonishment I found her standing not ten paces behind me.

"Girl!" I cried, "what are you doing here? I thought that you had gone to the cave, as I told you to do."

Up went her head, and the look that she gave me took all the majesty out of me, and left me feeling more like the palace janitor—if palaces have janitors.

"As you told me to do!" she cried, stamping her little foot. "I do as I please. I am the daughter of a king, and furthermore, I hate you."

I was dumbfounded—this was my thanks for saving her from Jubal! I turned and looked at the corpse. "May be that I saved you from a worse fate, old man," I said, but I guess it was lost on Dian, for she never seemed to notice it at all.

"Let us go to my cave," I said, "I am tired and hungry."

She followed along a pace behind me, neither of us speaking. I was too angry, and she evidently didn't care to converse with the lower orders. I was mad all the way through, as I had certainly felt that at least a word of thanks should have rewarded me, for I knew that even by her own standards, I must have done a very wonderful thing to have killed the redoubtable Jubal in a hand-to-hand encounter.

We had no difficulty in finding my lair, and then I went down into the valley and bowled over a small antelope, which I dragged up the steep ascent to the ledge before the door. Here we ate in silence. Occasionally I glanced at her, thinking that the sight of her tearing at raw flesh with her hands and teeth like some wild animal would cause a revulsion of my sentiments toward her; but to my surprise I found that she ate quite as daintily as the most civilized woman of my acquaintance, and finally I found myself gazing in foolish rapture at the beauties of her strong, white teeth. Such is love.

After our repast we went down to the river together and bathed our hands and faces, and then after drinking our fill went back to the cave. Without a word I crawled into the farthest corner and, curling up, was soon asleep.

When I awoke I found Dian sitting in the doorway looking out across the valley. As I came out she moved to one side to let me pass, but she had no word for me. I wanted to hate her, but I couldn't. Every time I looked at her something came up in my throat, so that I nearly choked. I had never been in love before, but I did not need any aid in diagnosing my case—I certainly had it and had it bad. God, how I loved that beautiful, disdainful, tantalizing, prehistoric girl!

After we had eaten again I asked Dian if she intended returning to her tribe now that Jubal was dead, but she shook her head sadly, and said that she did not dare, for there was still Jubal's brother to be considered—his oldest brother.

"What has he to do with it?" I asked. "Does he too want you, or has the option on you become a family heirloom, to be passed on down from generation to generation?"

She was not quite sure as to what I meant.

"It is probable," she said, "that they all will want revenge for the death of Jubal—there are seven of them—seven terrible men. Someone may have to kill them all, if I am to return to my people."

It began to look as though I had assumed a contract much too large for me—about seven sizes, in fact.

"Had Jubal any cousins?" I asked. It was just as well to know the worst at once.

"Yes," replied Dian, "but they don't count—they all have mates. Jubal's brothers have no mates because Jubal could get none for himself. He was so ugly that women ran away from him—some have even thrown themselves from the cliffs of Amoz into the Darel Az rather than mate with the Ugly One."

"But what had that to do with his brothers?" I asked.

"I forget that you are not of Pellucidar," said Dian, with a look of pity mixed with contempt, and the contempt seemed to be laid on a little thicker than the circumstance warranted—as though to make quite certain that I shouldn't overlook it. "You see," she continued, "a younger brother may not take a mate until all his older brothers have done so, unless the older brother waives his prerogative, which Jubal would not do, knowing that as long as he kept them single they would be all the keener in aiding him to secure a mate."

Noticing that Dian was becoming more communicative I began to entertain hopes that she might be warming up toward me a bit, although upon what slender thread I hung my hopes I soon discovered.

"As you dare not return to Amoz," I ventured, "what is to become of you since you cannot be happy here with me, hating me as you do?"

"I shall have to put up with you," she replied coldly, "until you see fit to go elsewhere and leave me in peace, then I shall get along very well alone."

I looked at her in utter amazement. It seemed incredible that even a prehistoric woman could be so cold and heartless and ungrateful. Then I arose.

"I shall leave you NOW," I said haughtily, "I have had quite enough of your ingratitude and your insults," and then I turned and strode majestically down toward the valley. I had taken a hundred steps in absolute silence, and then Dian spoke.

"I hate you!" she shouted, and her voice broke—in rage, I thought.

I was absolutely miserable, but I hadn't gone too far when I began to realize that I couldn't leave her alone there without protection, to hunt her own food amid the dangers of that savage world. She might hate me, and revile me, and heap indignity after indignity upon me, as she already had, until I should have hated her; but the pitiful fact remained that I loved her, and I couldn't leave her there alone.

The more I thought about it the madder I got, so that by the time I reached the valley I was furious, and the result of it was that I turned right around and went up that cliff again as fast as I had come down. I saw that Dian had left the ledge and gone within the cave, but I bolted right in after her. She was lying upon her face on the pile of grasses I had gathered for her bed. When she heard me enter she sprang to her feet like a tigress.

"I hate you!" she cried.

Coming from the brilliant light of the noonday sun into the semidarkness of the cave I could not see her features, and I was rather glad, for I disliked to think of the hate that I should have read there.

I never said a word to her at first. I just strode across the cave and grasped her by the wrists, and when she struggled, I put my arm around her so as to pinion her hands to her sides. She fought like a tigress, but I took my free hand and pushed her head back—I imagine that I had suddenly turned brute, that I had gone back a thousand million years, and was again a veritable cave man taking my mate by force—and then I kissed that beautiful mouth again and again.

"Dian," I cried, shaking her roughly, "I love you. Can't you understand that I love you? That I love you better than all else in this world or my own? That I am going to have you? That love like mine cannot be denied?"

I noticed that she lay very still in my arms now, and as my eyes became accustomed to the light I saw that she was smiling—a very contented, happy smile. I was thunderstruck. Then I realized that, very gently, she was trying to disengage her arms, and I loosened my grip upon them so that she could do so. Slowly they came up and stole about my neck, and then she drew my lips down to hers once more and held them there for a long time. At last she spoke.

"Why didn't you do this at first, David? I have been waiting so long."

"What!" I cried. "You said that you hated me!"

"Did you expect me to run into your arms, and say that I loved you before I knew that you loved me?" she asked.

"But I have told you right along that I love you," I said. "Love speaks in acts," she replied. "You could have made your mouth say what you wished it to say, but just now when you came and took me in your arms your heart spoke to mine in the language that a woman's heart understands. What a silly man you are, David."

"Then you haven't hated me at all, Dian?" I asked.

"I have loved you always," she whispered, "from the first moment that I saw you, although I did not know it until that time you struck down Hooja the Sly One, and then spurned me."

"But I didn't spurn you, dear," I cried. "I didn't know your ways—I doubt if I do now. It seems incredible that you could have reviled me so, and yet have cared for me all the time."

"You might have known," she said, "when I did not run away from you that it was not hate which chained me to you. While you were battling with Jubal, I could have run to the edge of the forest, and when I learned the outcome of the combat it would have been a simple thing to have eluded you and returned to my own people."

"But Jubal's brothers—and cousins—" I reminded her, "how about them?"

She smiled, and hid her face on my shoulder.

"I had to tell you SOMETHING, David," she whispered. "I must needs have SOME excuse for remaining near you."

"You little sinner!" I exclaimed. "And you have caused me all this anguish for nothing!"

"I have suffered even more," she answered simply, "for I thought that you did not love me, and I was helpless. I couldn't come to you and demand that my love be returned, as you have just come to me. Just now when you went away hope went with you. I was wretched, terrified, miserable, and my heart was breaking. I wept, and I have not done that before since my mother died," and now I saw that there was the moisture of tears about her eyes. It was near to making me cry myself when I thought of all that poor child had been through. Motherless and unprotected; hunted across a savage, primeval world by that hideous brute of a man; exposed to the attacks of the countless fearsome denizens of its mountains, its plains, and its jungles— it was a miracle that she had survived it all.

To me it was a revelation of the things my early forebears must have endured that the human race of the outer crust might survive. It made me very proud to think that I had won the love of such a woman. Of course she couldn't read or write; there was nothing cultured or refined about her as you judge culture and refinement; but she was the essence of all that is best in woman, for she was good, and brave, and noble, and virtuous. And she was all these things in spite of the fact that their observance entailed suffering and danger and possible death.

How much easier it would have been to have gone to Jubal in the first place! She would have been his lawful mate. She would have been queen in her own land—and it meant just as much to the cave woman to be a queen in the Stone Age as it does to the woman of today to be a queen now; it's all comparative glory any way you look at it, and if there were only half-naked savages on the outer crust today, you'd find that it would be considerable glory to be the wife of a Dahomey chief.

I couldn't help but compare Dian's action with that of a splendid young woman I had known in New York—I mean splendid to look at and to talk to. She had been head over heels in love with a chum of mine—a clean, manly chap—but she had married a broken-down, disreputable old debauchee because he was a count in some dinky little European principality that was not even accorded a distinctive color by Rand McNally.

Yes, I was mighty proud of Dian.

After a time we decided to set out for Sari, as I was anxious to see Perry, and to know that all was right with him. I had told Dian about our plan of emancipating the human race of Pellucidar, and she was fairly wild over it. She said that if Dacor, her brother, would only return he could easily be king of

Amoz, and that then he and Ghak could form an alliance. That would give us a flying start, for the Sarians and the Amozites were both very powerful tribes. Once they had been armed with swords, and bows and arrows, and trained in their use we were confident that they could overcome any tribe that seemed disinclined to join the great army of federated states with which we were planning to march upon the Mahars.

I explained the various destructive engines of war which Perry and I could construct after a little experimentation—gunpowder, rifles, cannon, and the like, and Dian would clap her hands, and throw her arms about my neck, and tell me what a wonderful thing I was. She was beginning to think that I was omnipotent although I really hadn't done anything but talk—but that is the way with women when they love. Perry used to say that if a fellow was one-tenth as remarkable as his wife or mother thought him, he would have the world by the tail with a down-hill drag.

The first time we started for Sari I stepped into a nest of poisonous vipers before we reached the valley. A little fellow stung me on the ankle, and Dian made me come back to the cave. She said that I mustn't exercise, or it might prove fatal—if it had been a full-grown snake that struck me she said, I wouldn't have moved a single pace from the nest—I'd have died in my tracks, so virulent is the poison. As it was I must have been laid up for quite a while, though Dian's poultices of herbs and leaves finally reduced the swelling and drew out the poison.

The episode proved most fortunate, however, as it gave me an idea which added a thousand-fold to the value of my arrows as missiles of offense and defense. As soon as I was able to be about again, I sought out some adult vipers of the species which had stung me, and having killed them, I extracted their virus, smearing it upon the tips of several arrows. Later I shot a hyaenodon with one of these, and though my arrow inflicted but a superficial flesh wound the beast crumpled in death almost immediately after he was hit.

We now set out once more for the land of the Sarians, and it was with feelings of sincere regret that we bade good-bye to our beautiful Garden of Eden, in the comparative peace and harmony of which we had lived the happiest moments of our lives. How long we had been there I did not know, for as I have told you, time had ceased to exist for me beneath that eternal noonday sun—it may have been an hour, or a month of earthly time; I do not know.

CHAPTER FIFTEEN
Back to Earth

WE CROSSED THE RIVER AND PASSED THROUGH THE mountains beyond, and finally we came out upon a great level plain which stretched away as far as the eye could reach. I cannot tell you in what direction it stretched even if you would care to know, for all the while that I was within Pellucidar I never discovered any but local methods of indicating direction—there is no north, no south, no east, no west. UP is about the only direction which is well defined, and that, of course, is DOWN to you of the outer crust. Since the sun neither rises nor sets there is no method of indicating direction beyond visible objects such as high mountains, forests, lakes, and seas.

The plain which lies beyond the white cliffs which flank the Darel Az upon the shore nearest the Mountains of the Clouds is about as near to any direction as any Pellucidarian can come. If you happen not to have heard of the Darel Az, or the white cliffs, or the Mountains of the Clouds you feel that there is something lacking, and long for the good old understandable northeast and southwest of the outer world.

We had barely entered the great plain when we discovered two enormous animals approaching us from a great distance. So far were they that we could not distinguish what manner of beasts they might be, but as they came closer, I saw that they were enormous quadrupeds, eighty or a hundred feet long, with tiny heads perched at the top of very long necks. Their heads must have been quite forty feet from the ground. The beasts moved very slowly—that is their action was slow—but their strides covered such a great distance that in reality they traveled considerably faster than a man walks.

As they drew still nearer we discovered that upon the back of each sat a human being. Then Dian knew what they were, though she never before had seen one.

"They are lidis from the land of the Thorians," she cried. "Thoria lies at the outer verge of the Land of Awful Shadow. The Thorians alone of all the races of Pellucidar ride the lidi, for nowhere else than beside the dark country are they found."

"What is the Land of Awful Shadow?" I asked.

"It is the land which lies beneath the Dead World," replied Dian; "the Dead World which hangs forever between the sun and Pellucidar above the Land of Awful Shadow. It is the Dead World which makes the great shadow upon this portion of Pellucidar."

I did not fully understand what she meant, nor am I sure that I do yet, for I have never been to that part of Pellucidar from which the Dead World is visible; but Perry says that it is the moon of Pellucidar—a tiny planet within a planet—and that it revolves around the earth's axis coincidently with the earth, and thus is always above the same spot within Pellucidar.

I remember that Perry was very much excited when I told him about this Dead World, for he seemed to think that it explained the hitherto inexplicable phenomena of nutation and the precession of the equinoxes.

When the two upon the lidis had come quite close to us we saw that one was a man and the other a woman. The former had held up his two hands, palms toward us, in sign of peace, and I had answered him in kind, when he suddenly gave a cry of astonishment and pleasure, and slipping from his enormous mount ran forward toward Dian, throwing his arms about her.

In an instant I was white with jealousy, but only for an instant; since Dian quickly drew the man toward me, telling him that I was David, her mate.

"And this is my brother, Dacor the Strong One, David," she said to me.

It appeared that the woman was Dacor's mate. He had found none to his liking among the Sari, nor farther on until he had come to the land of the Thoria, and there he had found and fought for this very lovely Thorian maiden whom he was bringing back to his own people.

When they had heard our story and our plans they decided to accompany us to Sari, that Dacor and Ghak might come to an agreement relative to an alliance, as Dacor was quite as enthusiastic about the proposed annihilation of the Mahars and Sagoths as either Dian or I.

After a journey which was, for Pellucidar, quite uneventful, we came to the first of the Sarian villages which consists of between one and two hundred artificial caves cut into the face of a great cliff. Here to our immense delight, we found both Perry and Ghak. The old man was quite overcome at sight of me for he had long since given me up as dead.

When I introduced Dian as my wife, he didn't quite know what to say, but he afterward remarked that with the pick of two worlds I could not have done better.

Ghak and Dacor reached a very amicable arrangement, and it was at a council of the head men of the various tribes of the Sari that the eventual form of government was tentatively agreed upon. Roughly, the various kingdoms were to remain virtually independent, but there was to be one great overlord, or emperor. It was decided that I should be the first of the dynasty of the emperors of Pellucidar.

We set about teaching the women how to make bows and arrows, and poison pouches. The young men hunted the vipers which provided the virus, and it was they who mined the iron ore, and fashioned the swords under Perry's direction. Rapidly the fever spread from one tribe to another until representatives from nations so far distant that the Sarians had never even heard of them came in to take the oath of allegiance which we required, and to learn the art of making the new weapons and using them.

We sent our young men out as instructors to every nation of the federation, and the movement had reached colossal proportions before the Mahars discovered it. The first intimation they had was when three of their great slave caravans were annihilated in rapid succession. They could not comprehend that the lower orders had suddenly developed a power which rendered them really formidable.

In one of the skirmishes with slave caravans some of our Sarians took a number of Sagoth prisoners, and among them were two who had been members of the guards within the building where we had been confined at Phutra. They told us that the Mahars were frantic with rage when they discovered what had taken place in the cellars of the buildings. The Sagoths knew that something very terrible had befallen their masters, but the Mahars had been most careful to see that no inkling of the true nature of their vital affliction reached beyond their own race. How long it would take for the race to become extinct it was impossible even to guess; but that this must eventually happen seemed inevitable.

The Mahars had offered fabulous rewards for the capture of any one of us alive, and at the same time had threatened to inflict the direst punishment upon whomever should harm us. The Sagoths could not understand these seemingly paradoxical instructions, though their purpose was quite evident to me. The Mahars wanted the Great Secret, and they knew that we alone could deliver it to them.

Perry's experiments in the manufacture of gunpowder and the fashioning of rifles had not progressed as rapidly as we had hoped—there was a whole lot about these two arts which Perry didn't know. We were both assured that the solution of these problems would advance the cause of civilization within Pellucidar thousands of years at a single stroke. Then there were various other arts and sciences which we wished to introduce, but our combined knowledge of them did not embrace the mechanical details which alone could render them of commercial, or practical value.

"David," said Perry, immediately after his latest failure to produce gunpowder that would even burn, "one of us must return to the outer world and bring back the information we lack. Here we have all the labor and materials for reproducing anything that ever has been produced above—what we lack is knowledge. Let us go back and get that knowledge in the shape of books—then this world will indeed be at our feet."

And so it was decided that I should return in the prospector, which still lay upon the edge of the forest at the point where we had first penetrated to the surface of the inner world. Dian would not listen to any arrangement for my going which did not include her, and I was not sorry that she wished to accompany me, for I wanted her to see my world, and I wanted my world to see her.

With a large force of men we marched to the great iron mole, which Perry soon had hoisted into position with its nose pointed back toward the outer crust. He went over all the machinery carefully. He replenished the air tanks, and manufactured oil for the engine. At last everything was ready, and we were about to set out when our pickets, a long, thin line of which had surrounded our camp at all times, reported that a great body of what appeared to be Sagoths and Mahars were approaching from the direction of Phutra.

Dian and I were ready to embark, but I was anxious to witness the first clash between two fair-sized armies of the opposing races of Pellucidar. I realized that this was to mark the historic beginning of a mighty struggle for possession of a world, and as the first emperor of Pellucidar I felt that it was not alone my duty, but my right, to be in the thick of that momentous struggle.

As the opposing army approached we saw that there were many Mahars with the Sagoth troops—an indication of the vast importance which the dominant race placed upon the outcome of this campaign, for it was not customary with them to take active part in the sorties which their creatures made for slaves—the only form of warfare which they waged upon the lower orders.

Ghak and Dacor were both with us, having come primarily to view the prospector. I placed Ghak with some of his Sarians on the right of our battle line. Dacor took the left, while I commanded the center. Behind us I stationed a sufficient reserve under one of Ghak's head men. The Sagoths advanced steadily with menacing spears, and I let them come until they were within easy bowshot before I gave the word to fire.

At the first volley of poison-tipped arrows the front ranks of the gorilla-men crumpled to the ground; but those behind charged over the prostrate forms of their comrades in a wild, mad rush to be upon us with their spears. A second volley stopped them for an instant, and then my reserve sprang through the openings in the firing line to engage them with sword and shield. The clumsy spears of the Sagoths were no match for the swords of the Sarian and Amozite, who turned the spear thrusts aside with their shields and leaped to close quarters with their lighter, handier weapons.

Ghak took his archers along the enemy's flank, and while the swordsmen engaged them in front, he poured volley after volley into their unprotected left. The Mahars did little real fighting, and were more in the way than otherwise, though occasionally one of them would fasten its powerful jaw upon the arm or leg of a Sarian.

The battle did not last a great while, for when Dacor and I led our men in upon the Sagoth's right with naked swords they were already so demoralized that they turned and fled before us. We pursued them for some time, taking many prisoners and recovering nearly a hundred slaves, among whom was Hooja the Sly One.

He told me that he had been captured while on his way to his own land; but that his life had been spared in hope that through him the Mahars would learn the whereabouts of their Great Secret. Ghak and I were inclined to think that the Sly One had been guiding this expedition to the land of Sari, where he thought that the book might be found in Perry's possession; but we had no proof of this and so we took him in and treated him as one of us, although none liked him. And how he rewarded my generosity you will presently learn.

There were a number of Mahars among our prisoners, and so fearful were our own people of them that they would not approach them unless completely covered from the sight of the reptiles by a piece of skin. Even Dian shared the popular superstition regarding the evil effects of exposure to the eyes of angry Mahars, and though I laughed at her fears I was willing enough to humor them if it would relieve her apprehension in any degree, and so she sat apart from the prospector, near which the Mahars had been chained, while Perry and I again inspected every portion of the mechanism.

At last I took my place in the driving seat, and called to one of the men without to fetch Dian. It happened that Hooja stood quite close to the doorway of the prospector, so that it was he who, without my knowledge, went to bring her; but how he succeeded in accomplishing the fiendish thing he did, I cannot guess, unless there were others in the plot to aid him. Nor can I believe that, since all my people were loyal to me and would have made short work of Hooja had he suggested the heartless scheme, even had he had time to acquaint another with it. It was all done so quickly that I may only believe that it was the result of sudden impulse, aided by a number of, to Hooja, fortuitous circumstances occurring at precisely the right moment.

All I know is that it was Hooja who brought Dian to the prospector, still wrapped from head to toe in the skin of an enormous cave lion which covered her since the Mahar prisoners had been brought into camp. He deposited his burden in the seat beside me. I was all ready to get under way. The good-byes had been said. Perry had grasped my hand in the last, long farewell. I closed and barred the outer and inner doors, took my seat again at the driving mechanism, and pulled the starting lever.

As before on that far-gone night that had witnessed our first trial of the iron monster, there was a frightful roaring beneath us—the giant frame trembled and vibrated—there was a rush of sound as the loose earth passed up through the hollow space between the inner and outer jackets to be deposited in our wake. Once more the thing was off.

But on the instant of departure I was nearly thrown from my seat by the sudden lurching of the prospector. At first I did not realize what had happened, but presently it dawned upon me that just before entering the crust the towering body had fallen through its supporting scaffolding, and that instead of entering the ground vertically we were plunging into it at a different angle. Where it would bring us out upon the upper crust I could not even conjecture. And then I turned to note the effect of this strange experience upon Dian. She still sat shrouded in the great skin.

"Come, come," I cried, laughing, "come out of your shell. No Mahar eyes can reach you here," and I leaned over and snatched the lion skin from her. And then I shrank back upon my seat in utter horror.

The thing beneath the skin was not Dian—it was a hideous Mahar. Instantly I realized the trick that Hooja had played upon me, and the purpose of it. Rid of me, forever as he doubtless thought, Dian would be at his mercy. Frantically I tore at the steering wheel in an effort to turn the prospector back toward Pellucidar; but, as on that other occasion, I could not budge the thing a hair.

It is needless to recount the horrors or the monotony of that journey. It varied but little from the former one which had brought us from the outer to the inner world. Because of the angle at which we had entered the ground the trip required nearly a day longer, and brought me out here upon the sand of the Sahara instead of in the United States as I had hoped.

For months I have been waiting here for a white man to come. I dared not leave the prospector for fear I should never be able to find it again—the shifting sands of the desert would soon cover it, and then my only hope of returning to my Dian and her Pellucidar would be gone forever.

That I ever shall see her again seems but remotely possible, for how may I know upon what part of Pellucidar my return journey may terminate—and how, without a north or south or an east or a west may I hope ever to find my way across that vast world to the tiny spot where my lost love lies grieving for me?

That is the story as David Innes told it to me in the goat-skin tent upon the rim of the great Sahara Desert. The next day he took me out to see the prospector—it was precisely as he had described it. So huge was it that it could have been brought to this inaccessible part of the world by no means of transportation that existed there—it could only have come in the way that David Innes said it came—up through the crust of the earth from the inner world of Pellucidar.

I spent a week with him, and then, abandoning my lion hunt, returned directly to the coast and hurried to London where I purchased a great quantity of stuff which he wished to take back to Pellucidar with him. There were books, rifles, revolvers, ammunition, cameras, chemicals, telephones, telegraph instruments, wire, tools and more books—books upon every subject under the sun. He said he wanted a library with which they could reproduce the wonders of the twentieth century in the Stone Age and if quantity counts for anything I got it for him.

I took the things back to Algeria myself, and accompanied them to the end of the railroad; but from here I was recalled to America upon important business. However, I was able to employ a very trustworthy man to take charge of the caravan—the same guide, in fact, who had accompanied me on the previous trip into the Sahara—and after writing a long letter to

Innes in which I gave him my American address, I saw the expedition head south.

Among the other things which I sent to Innes was over five hundred miles of double, insulated wire of a very fine gauge. I had it packed on a special reel at his suggestion, as it was his idea that he could fasten one end here before he left and by paying it out through the end of the prospector lay a telegraph line between the outer and inner worlds. In my letter I told him to be sure to mark the terminus of the line very plainly with a high cairn, in case I was not able to reach him before he set out, so that I might easily find and communicate with him should he be so fortunate as to reach Pellucidar.

I received several letters from him after I returned to America—in fact he took advantage of every northward-passing caravan to drop me word of some sort. His last letter was written the day before he intended to depart. Here it is.

MY DEAR FRIEND:

Tomorrow I shall set out in quest of Pellucidar and Dian. That is if the Arabs don't get me. They have been very nasty of late. I don't know the cause, but on two occasions they have threatened my life. One, more friendly than the rest, told me today that they intended attacking me tonight. It would be unfortunate should anything of that sort happen now that I am so nearly ready to depart.

However, maybe I will be as well off, for the nearer the hour approaches, the slenderer my chances for success appear.

Here is the friendly Arab who is to take this letter north for me, so good-bye, and God bless you for your kindness to me.

The Arab tells me to hurry, for he sees a cloud of sand to the south—he thinks it is the party coming to murder me, and he doesn't want to be found with me. So good-bye again.

Yours,
DAVID INNES.

A year later found me at the end of the railroad once more, headed for the spot where I had left Innes. My first disappointment was when I discovered that my old guide had died within a few weeks of my return, nor could I find any member of my former party who could lead me to the same spot.

For months I searched that scorching land, interviewing countless desert sheiks in the hope that at last I might find one who had heard of Innes and his wonderful iron mole. Constantly my eyes scanned the blinding waste of sand for the rocky cairn beneath which I was to find the wires leading to Pellucidar—but always was I unsuccessful.

And always do these awful questions harass me when I think of David Innes and his strange adventures.

Did the Arabs murder him, after all, just on the eve of his departure? Or, did he again turn the nose of his iron monster toward the inner world? Did he reach it, or lies he somewhere buried in the heart of the great crust? And if he did come again to Pellucidar was it to break through into the bottom of one of her great island seas, or among some savage race far, far from the land of his heart's desire?

Does the answer lie somewhere upon the bosom of the broad Sahara, at the end of two tiny wires, hidden beneath a lost cairn? I wonder.

THE END